BIRD·BOY

VOLUME I: THE SWORD OF MALI MANI

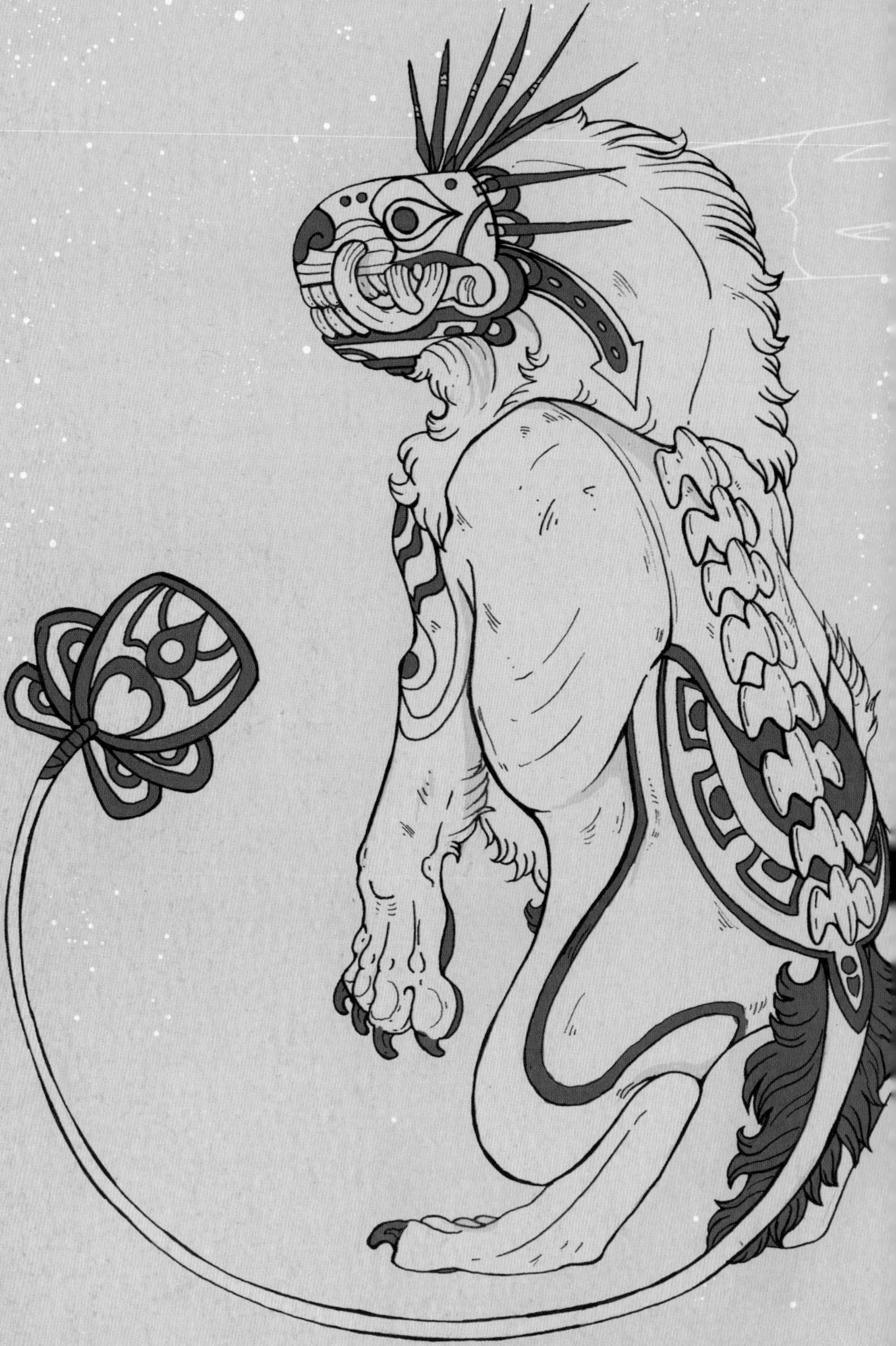

BIRD·BOY ™

VOLUME I: THE SWORD OF MALI MANI

Written and illustrated by
Anne Szabla

DARK HORSE BOOKS

President and Publisher
Mike Richardson

Editor
Scott Allie

Associate Editor
Shantel LaRocque

Assistant Editor
Katii O'Brien

Collection Designer
Sandy Tanaka

Digital Art Technician
Christianne Goudreau

Neil Hankerson Executive Vice President • Tom Weddle Chief Financial Officer • Randy Stradley Vice President of Publishing • Michael Martens Vice President of Book Trade Sales • Matt Parkinson Vice President of Marketing • David Scroggy Vice President of Product Development • Dale LaFountain Vice President of Information Technology • Cara Niece Vice President of Production and Scheduling • Ken Lizzi General Counsel • Davey Estrada Editorial Director • Dave Marshall Editor in Chief • Scott Allie Executive Senior Editor • Chris Warner Senior Books Editor • Cary Grazzini Director of Print and Development • Lia Ribacchi Art Director • Mark Bernardi Director of Digital Publishing

Published by Dark Horse Books
A division of Dark Horse Comics, Inc.
10956 SE Main Street
Milwaukie, OR 97222

First edition: May 2016
ISBN 978-1-61655-930-4

1 3 5 7 9 10 8 6 4 2
Printed in China

Bird-Boy.com

International Licensing: (503) 905-2377 Comic Shop Locator Service: (888) 266-4226

Names: Szabla, Anne, author, illustrator.
Title: Bird boy. Volume 1, The sword of Mali Mani / written and illustrated
  by Anne Szabla.
Other titles: Sword of Mali Mani
Description: First edition. | Milwaukie, OR : Dark Horse Books, 2016. |
  Summary: Ten-year-old Bali tries to prove his worth to his Northern tribe by
  setting out into the forbidden forest where he finds the legendary sword
  of Mali Mani and fights his way home across a dangerous land of gods, men,
  and beasts.
Identifiers: LCCN 2015046427 | ISBN 9781616559304 (paperback)
Subjects: LCSH: Graphic novels. | CYAC: Graphic novels. | Fantasy. | BISAC:
  JUVENILE FICTION / Comics & Graphic Novels / General.
Classification: LCC PZ7.7.S98 Bi 2016 | DDC 741.5/973–dc23
LC record available at http://lccn.loc.gov/2015046427

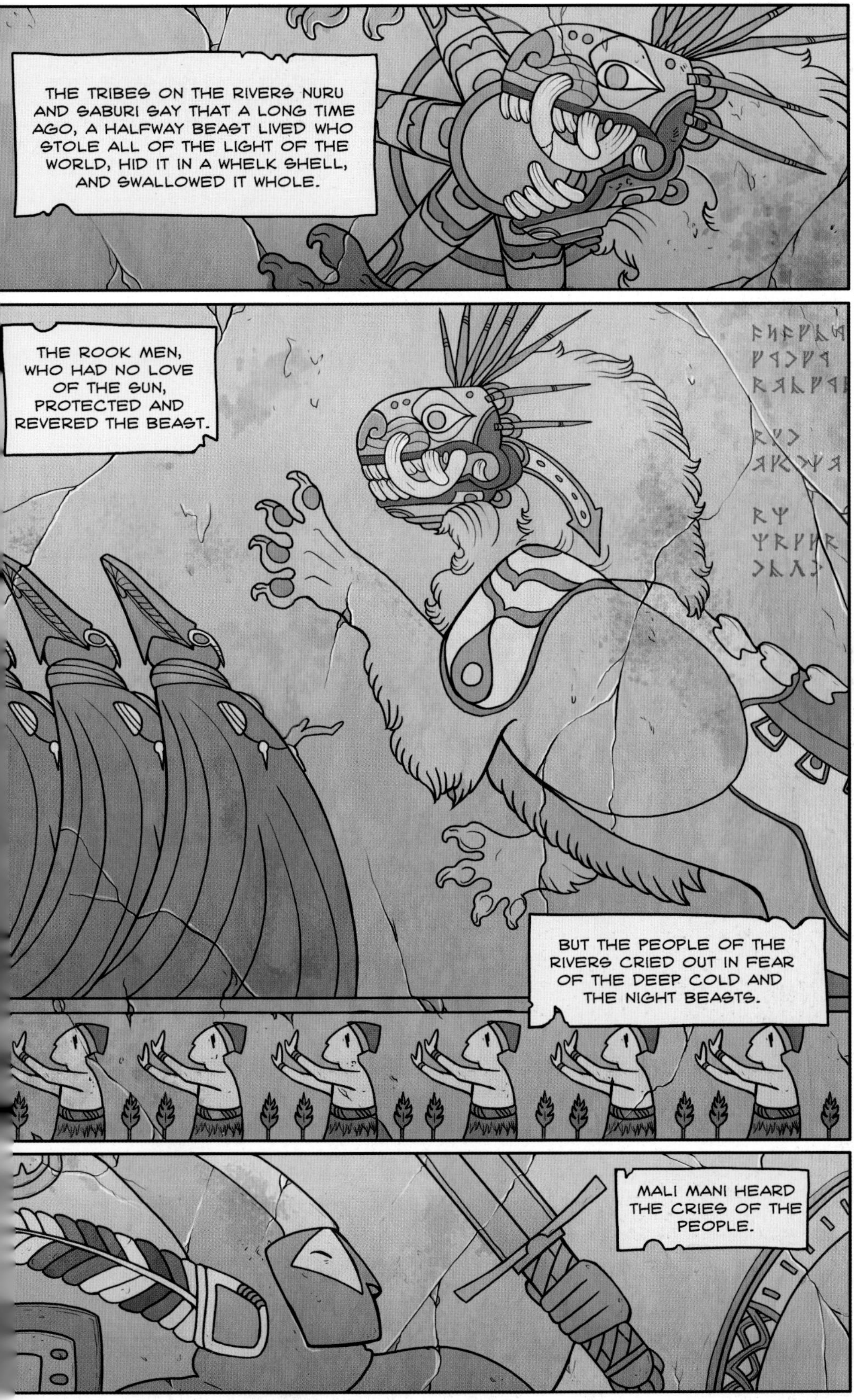
THE TRIBES ON THE RIVERS NURU AND SABURI SAY THAT A LONG TIME AGO, A HALFWAY BEAST LIVED WHO STOLE ALL OF THE LIGHT OF THE WORLD, HID IT IN A WHELK SHELL, AND SWALLOWED IT WHOLE.
THE ROOK MEN, WHO HAD NO LOVE OF THE SUN, PROTECTED AND REVERED THE BEAST.
BUT THE PEOPLE OF THE RIVERS CRIED OUT IN FEAR OF THE DEEP COLD AND THE NIGHT BEASTS.
MALI MANI HEARD THE CRIES OF THE PEOPLE.

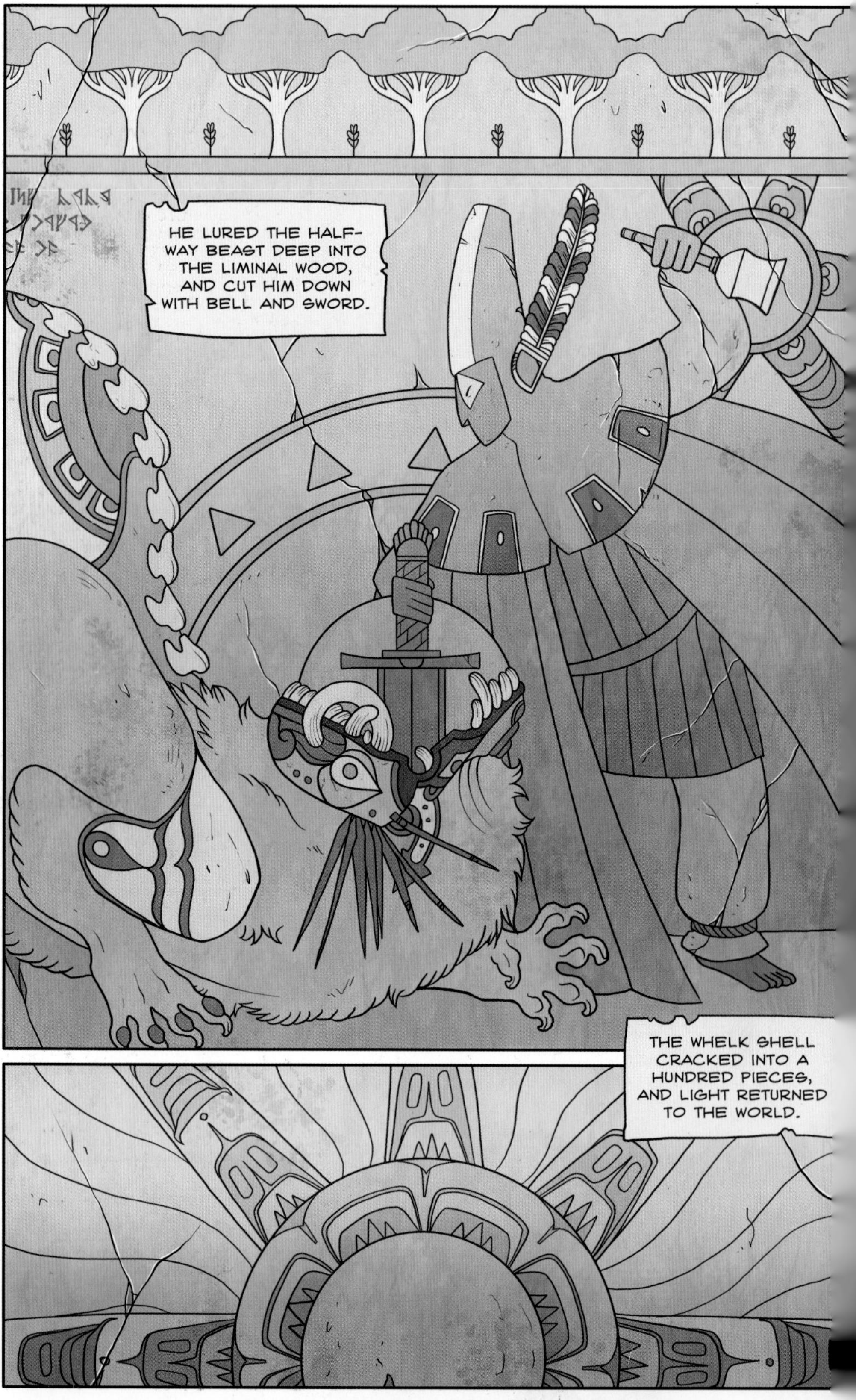
HE LURED THE HALF-WAY BEAST DEEP INTO THE LIMINAL WOOD, AND CUT HIM DOWN WITH BELL AND SWORD.
THE WHELK SHELL CRACKED INTO A HUNDRED PIECES, AND LIGHT RETURNED TO THE WORLD.

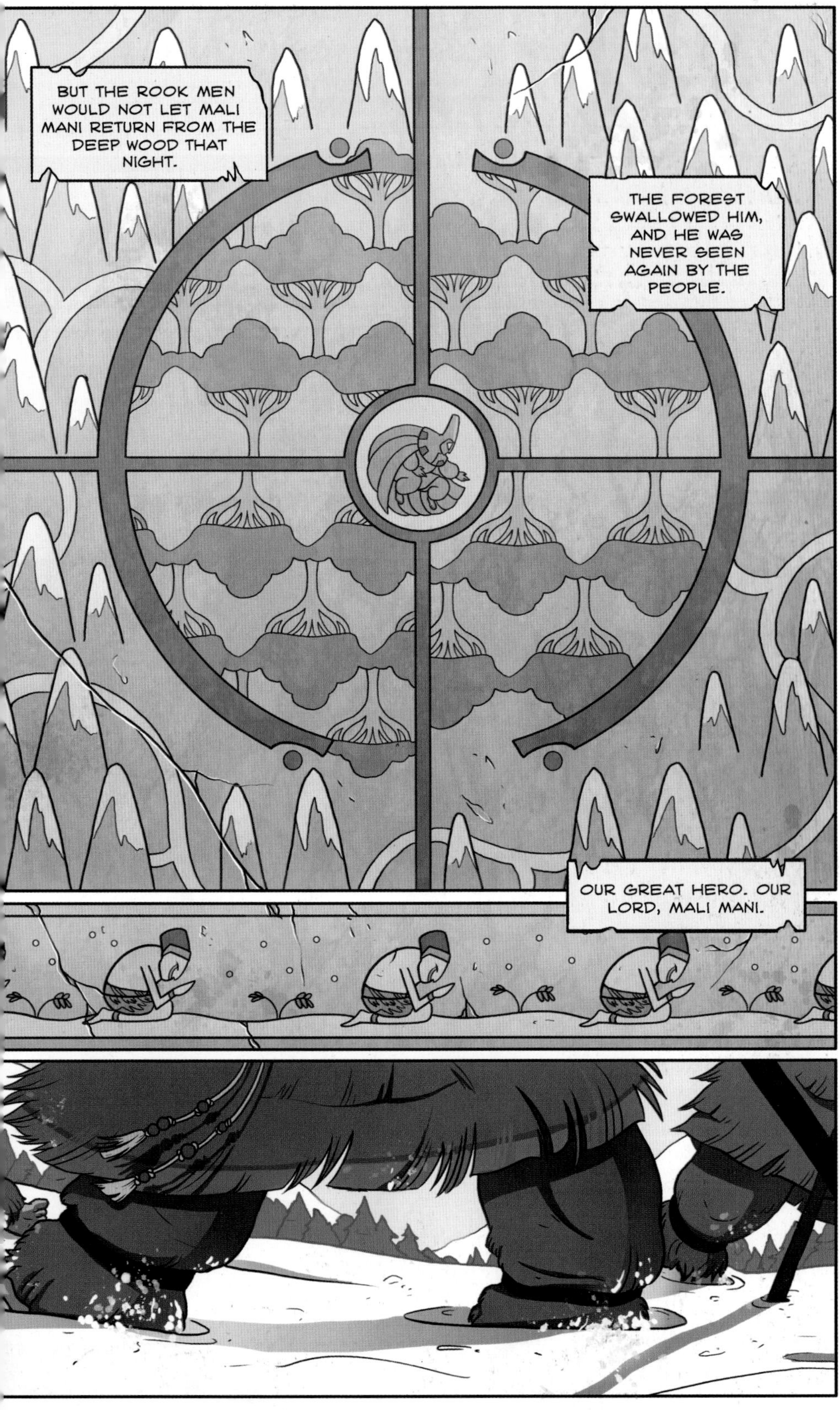
BUT THE ROOK MEN WOULD NOT LET MALI MANI RETURN FROM THE DEEP WOOD THAT NIGHT.
THE FOREST SWALLOWED HIM, AND HE WAS NEVER SEEN AGAIN BY THE PEOPLE.
OUR GREAT HERO. OUR LORD, MALI MANI.

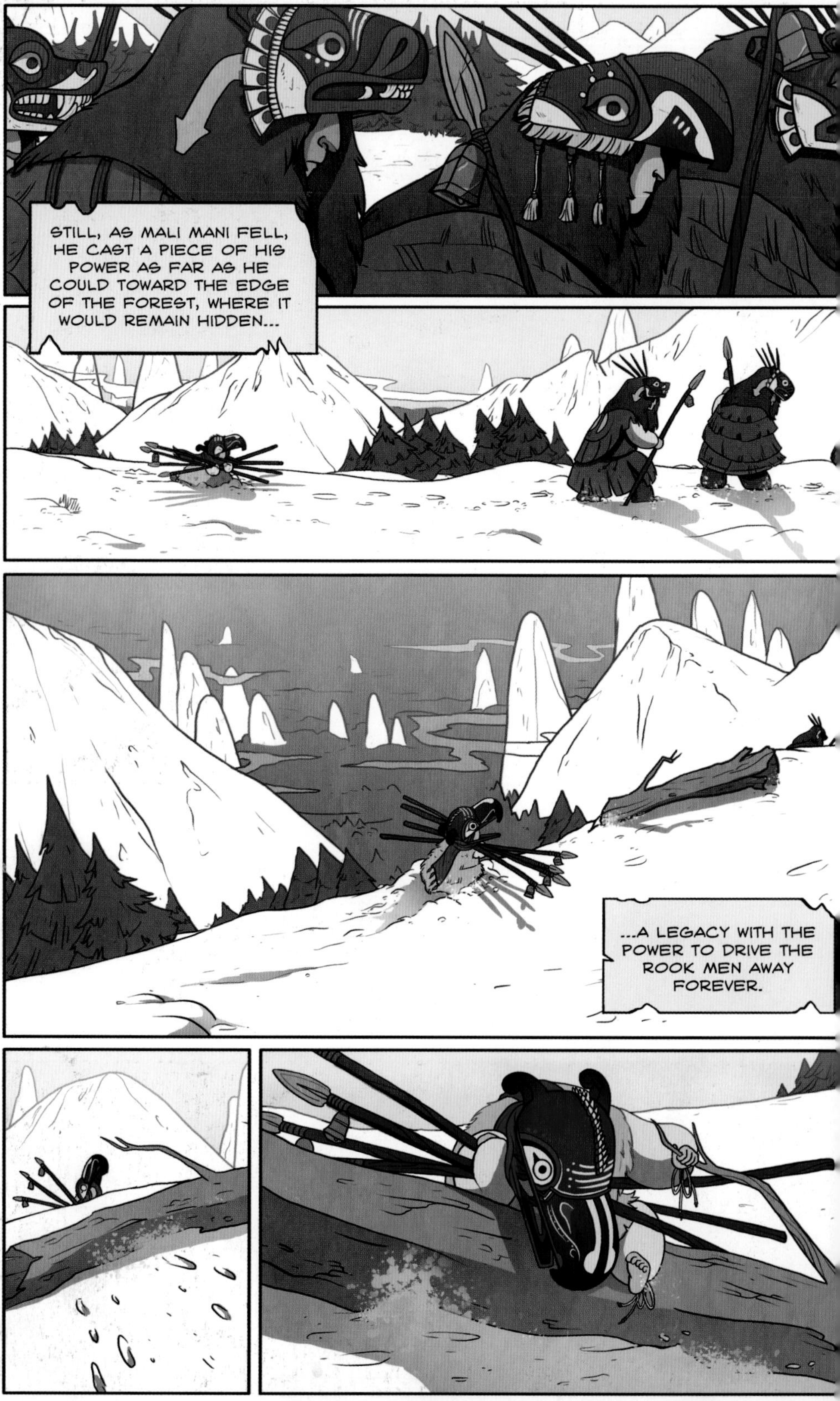
STILL, AS MALI MANI FELL, HE CAST A PIECE OF HIS POWER AS FAR AS HE COULD TOWARD THE EDGE OF THE FOREST, WHERE IT WOULD REMAIN HIDDEN...
...A LEGACY WITH THE POWER TO DRIVE THE ROOK MEN AWAY FOREVER.

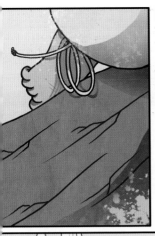

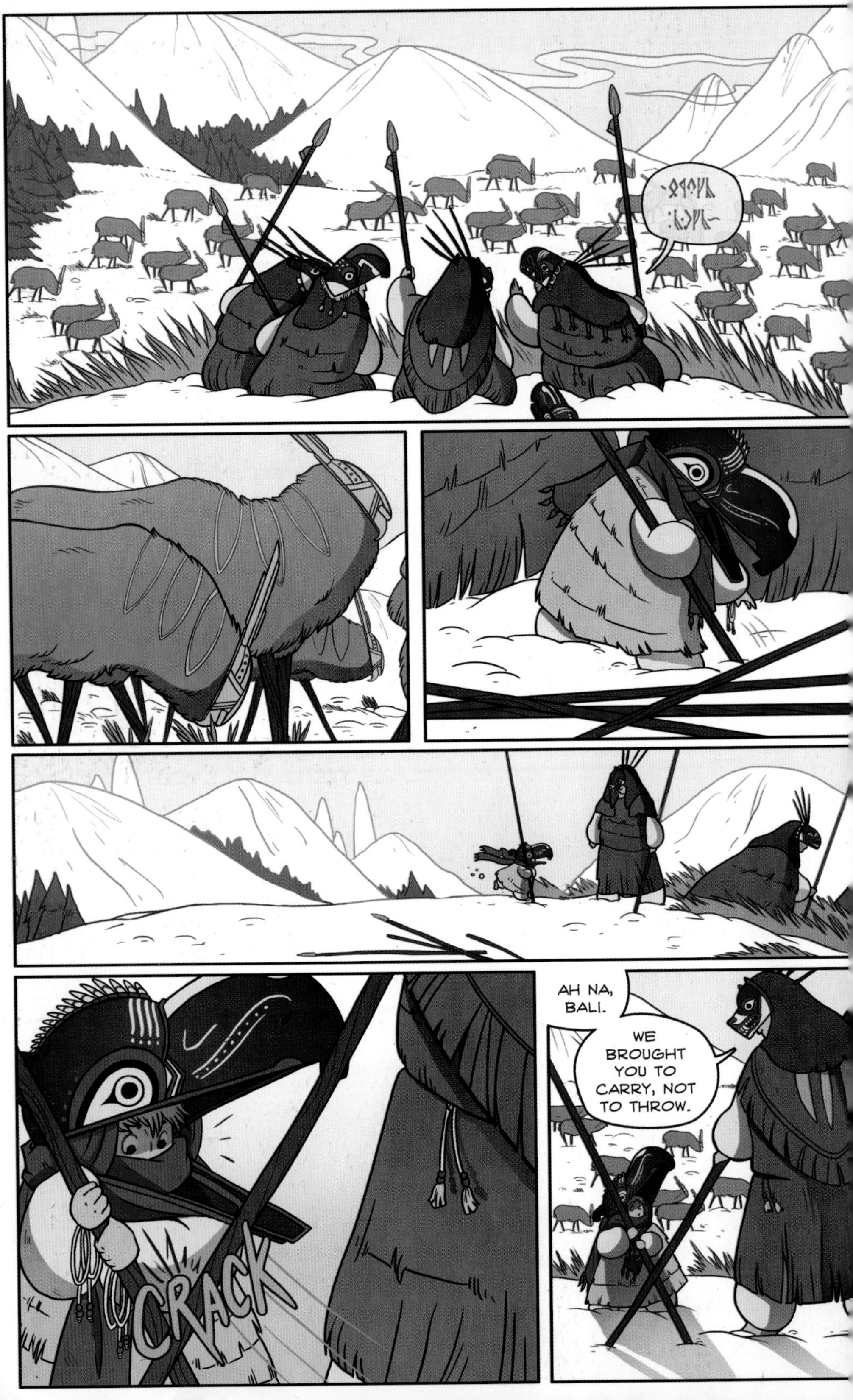
CRACK
AH NA, BALI.
WE BROUGHT YOU TO CARRY, NOT TO THROW.

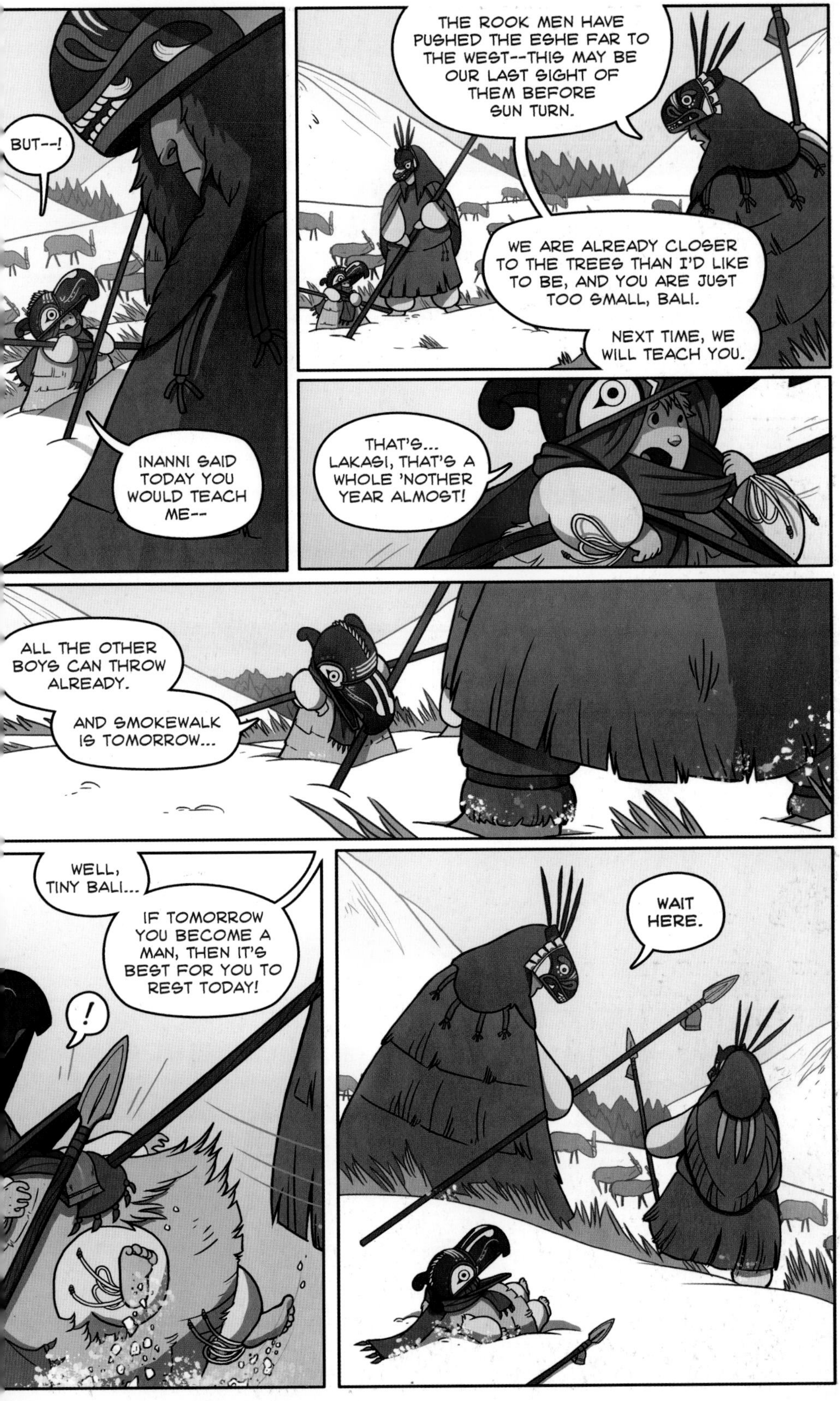
BUT--!
THE ROOK MEN HAVE PUSHED THE ESHE FAR TO THE WEST--THIS MAY BE OUR LAST SIGHT OF THEM BEFORE SUN TURN.
WE ARE ALREADY CLOSER TO THE TREES THAN I'D LIKE TO BE, AND YOU ARE JUST TOO SMALL, BALI.
NEXT TIME, WE WILL TEACH YOU.
INANNI SAID TODAY YOU WOULD TEACH ME--
THAT'S... LAKASI, THAT'S A WHOLE 'NOTHER YEAR ALMOST!
ALL THE OTHER BOYS CAN THROW ALREADY.
AND SMOKEWALK IS TOMORROW...
WELL, TINY BALI...
IF TOMORROW YOU BECOME A MAN, THEN IT'S BEST FOR YOU TO REST TODAY!
!
WAIT HERE.

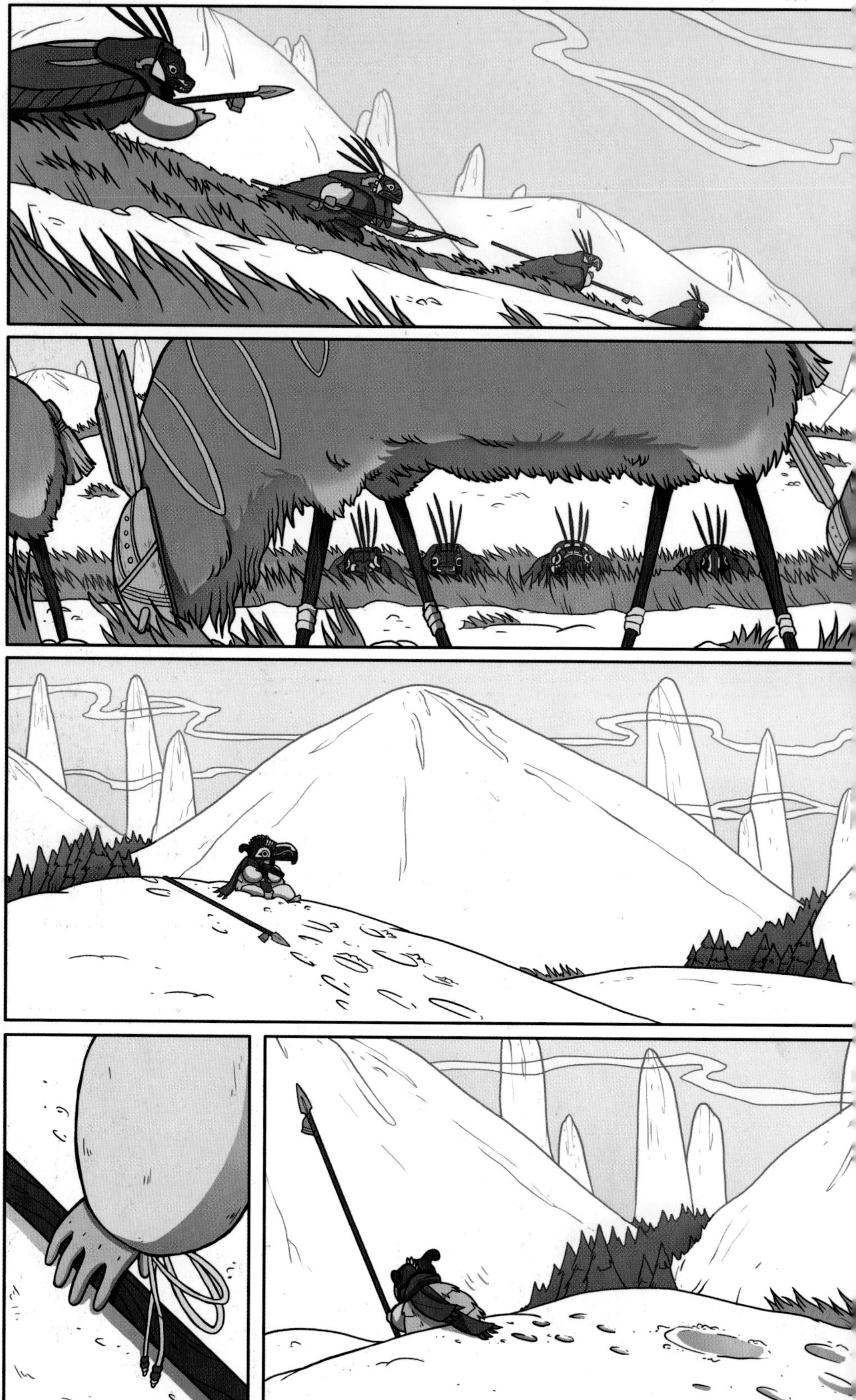

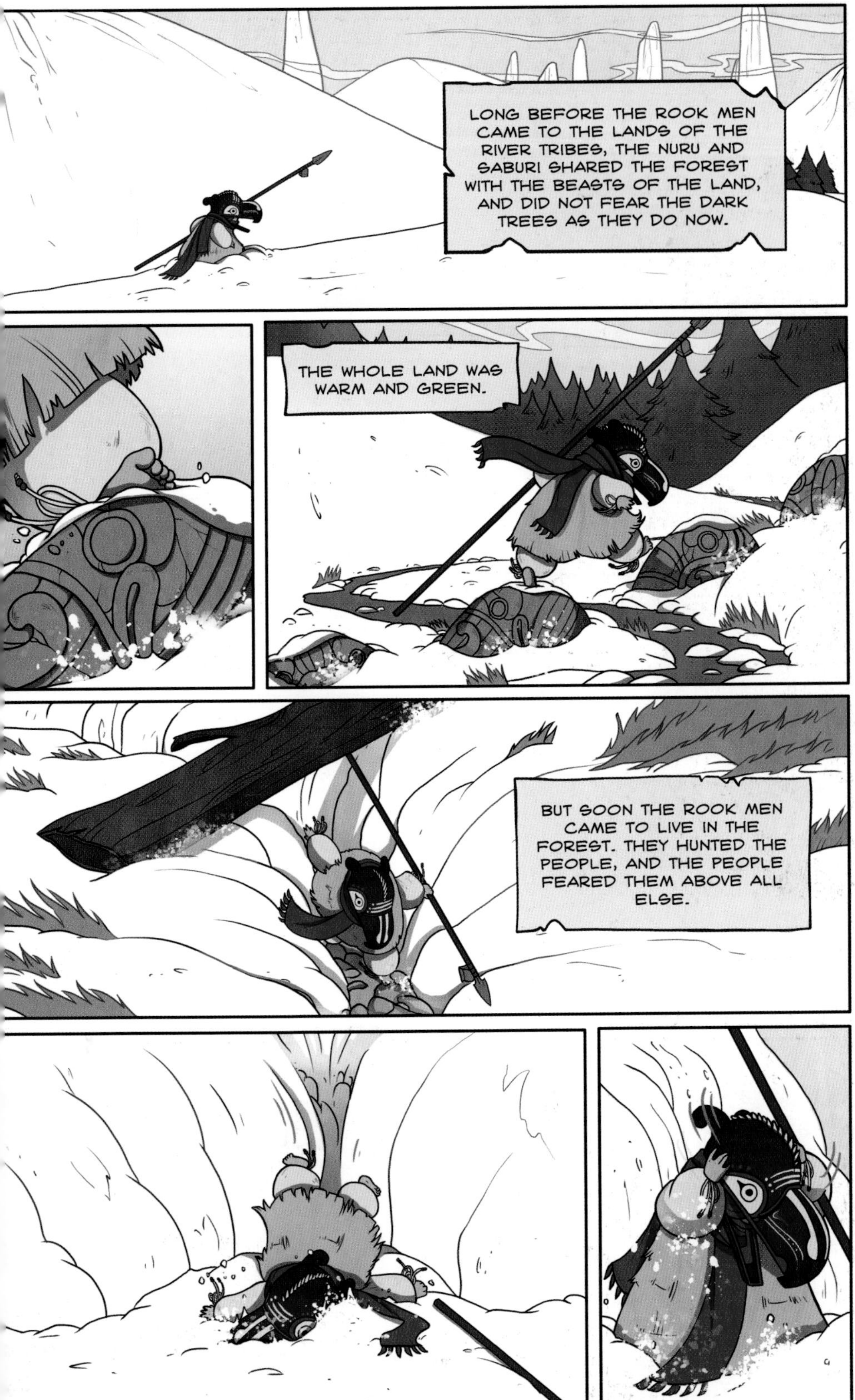
LONG BEFORE THE ROOK MEN CAME TO THE LANDS OF THE RIVER TRIBES, THE NURU AND SABURI SHARED THE FOREST WITH THE BEASTS OF THE LAND, AND DID NOT FEAR THE DARK TREES AS THEY DO NOW.
THE WHOLE LAND WAS WARM AND GREEN.
BUT SOON THE ROOK MEN CAME TO LIVE IN THE FOREST. THEY HUNTED THE PEOPLE, AND THE PEOPLE FEARED THEM ABOVE ALL ELSE.

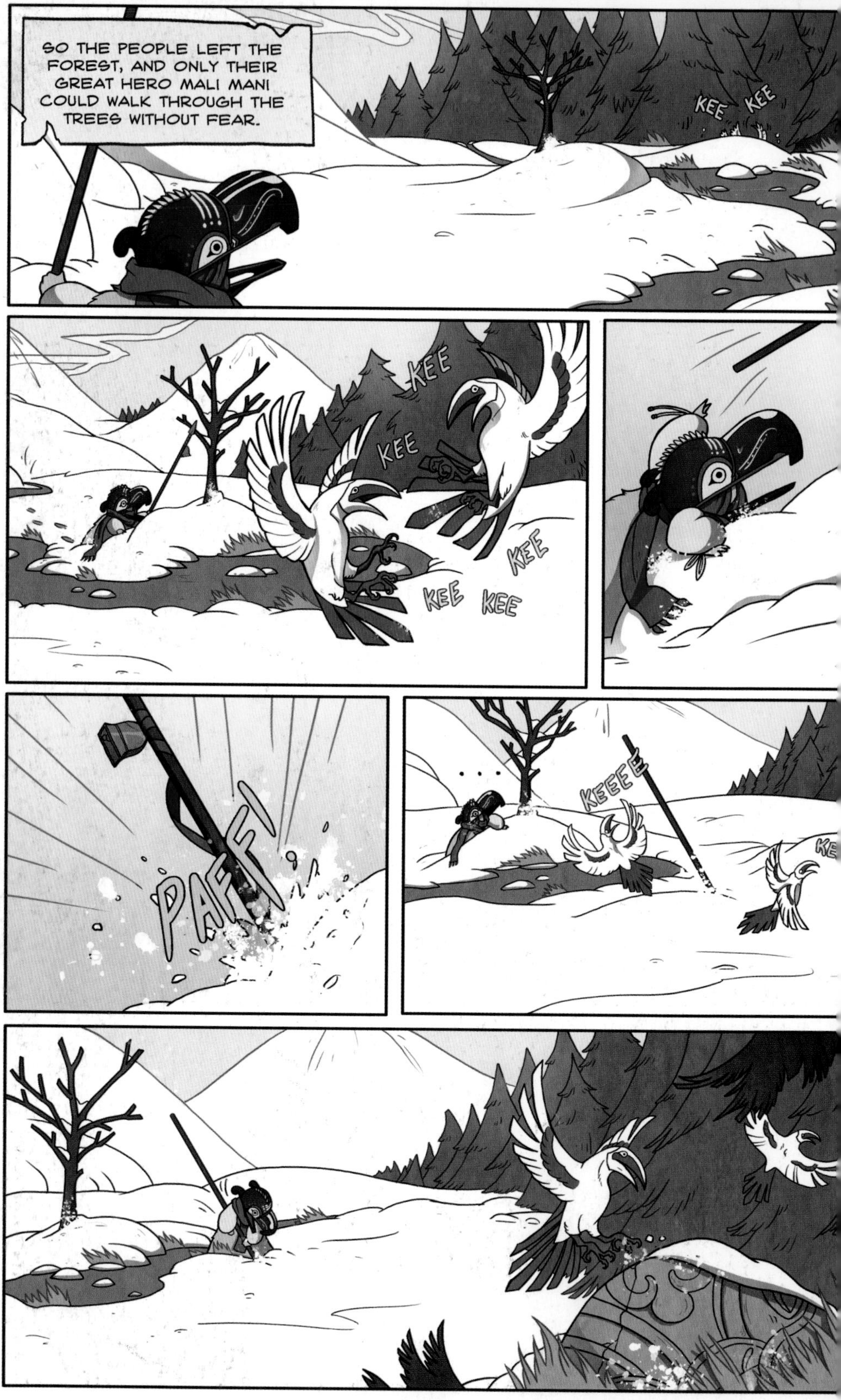
SO THE PEOPLE LEFT THE FOREST, AND ONLY THEIR GREAT HERO MALI MANI COULD WALK THROUGH THE TREES WITHOUT FEAR.
KEE KEE
KEE
KEE
KEE
KEE KEE
PAFF!
. . .
KEEEE

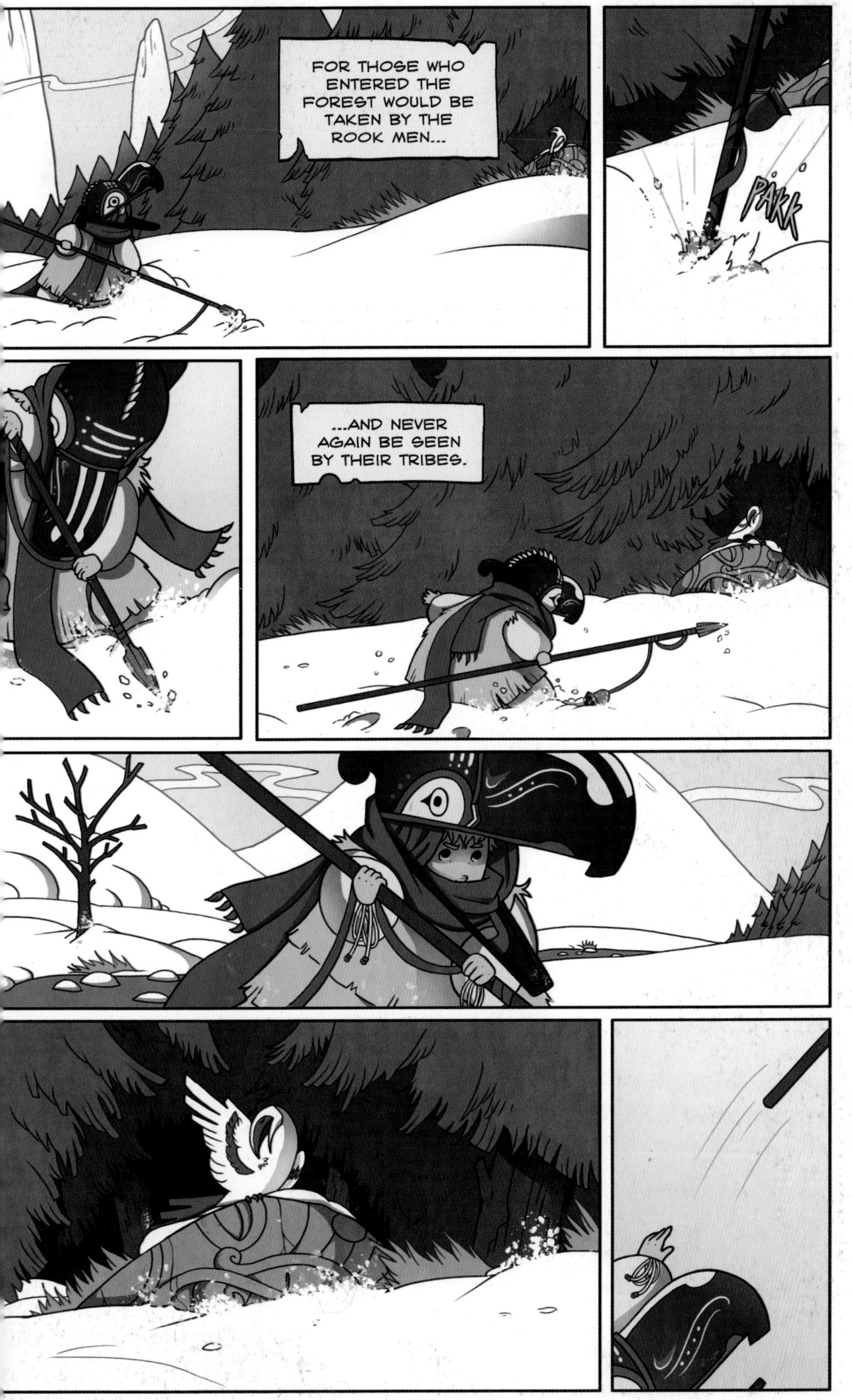
FOR THOSE WHO ENTERED THE FOREST WOULD BE TAKEN BY THE ROOK MEN...
PAKK
...AND NEVER AGAIN BE SEEN BY THEIR TRIBES.

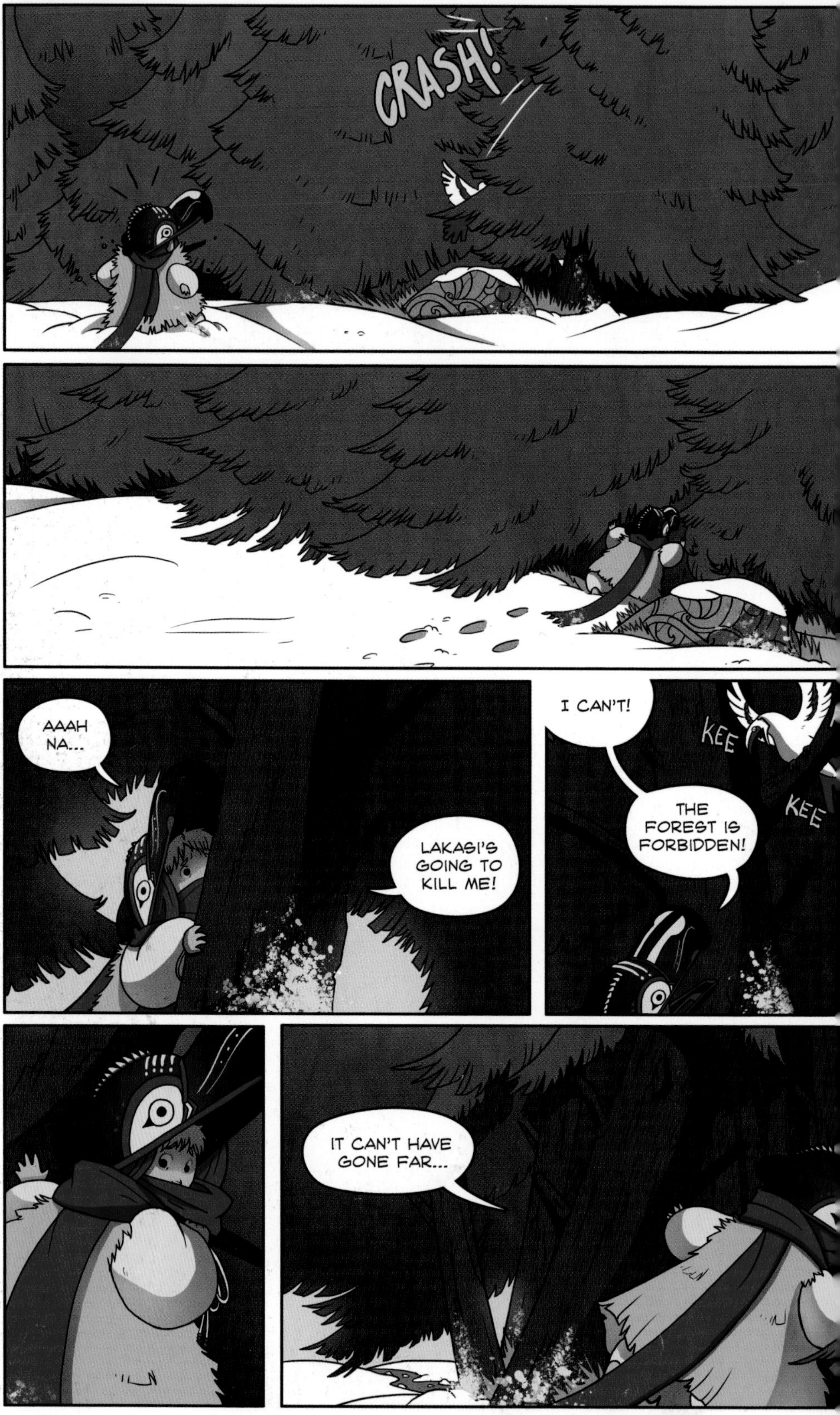
CRASH!
AAAH NA...
LAKASI'S GOING TO KILL ME!
I CAN'T!
KEE
KEE
THE FOREST IS FORBIDDEN!
IT CAN'T HAVE GONE FAR...

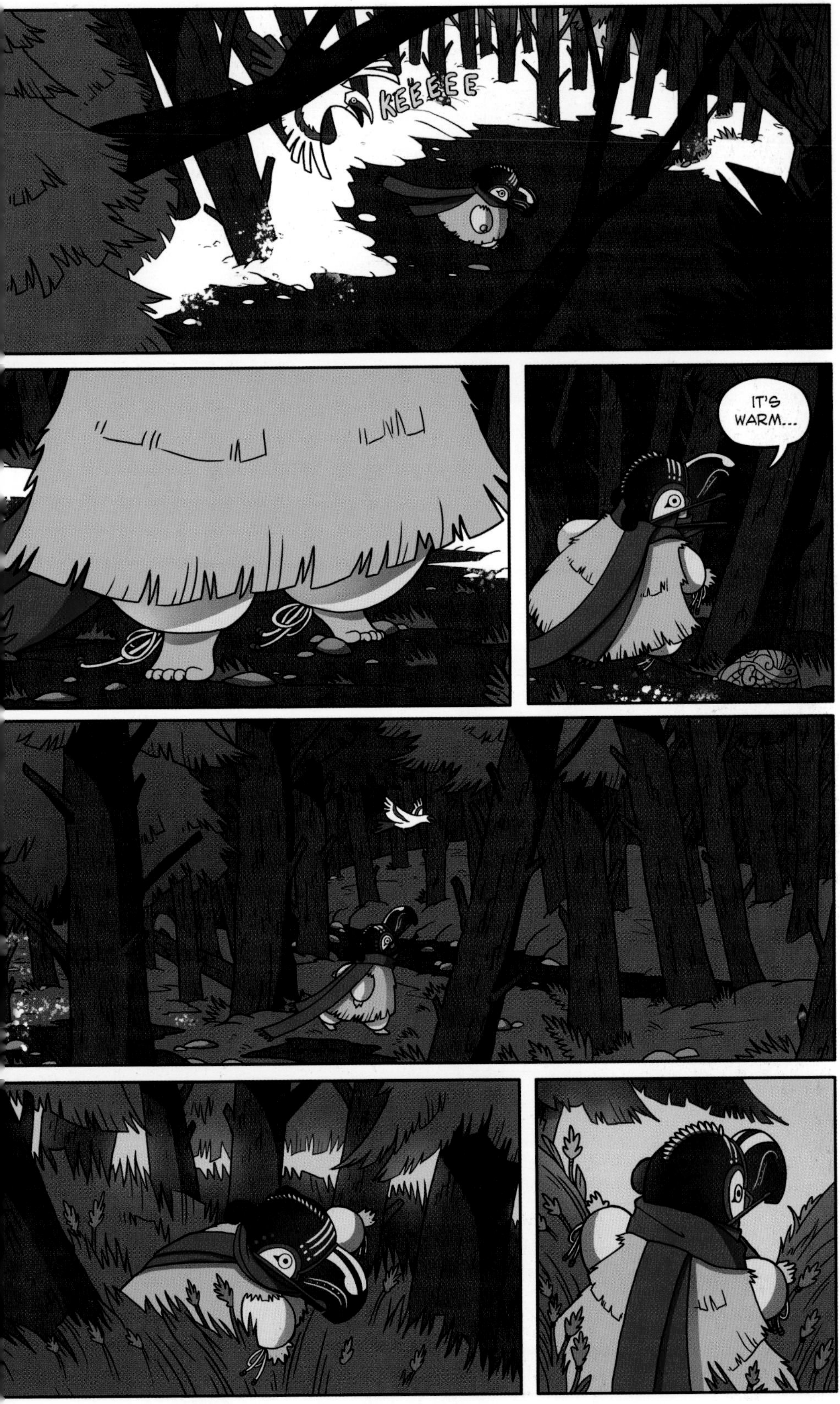
KEEEEE
IT'S WARM...

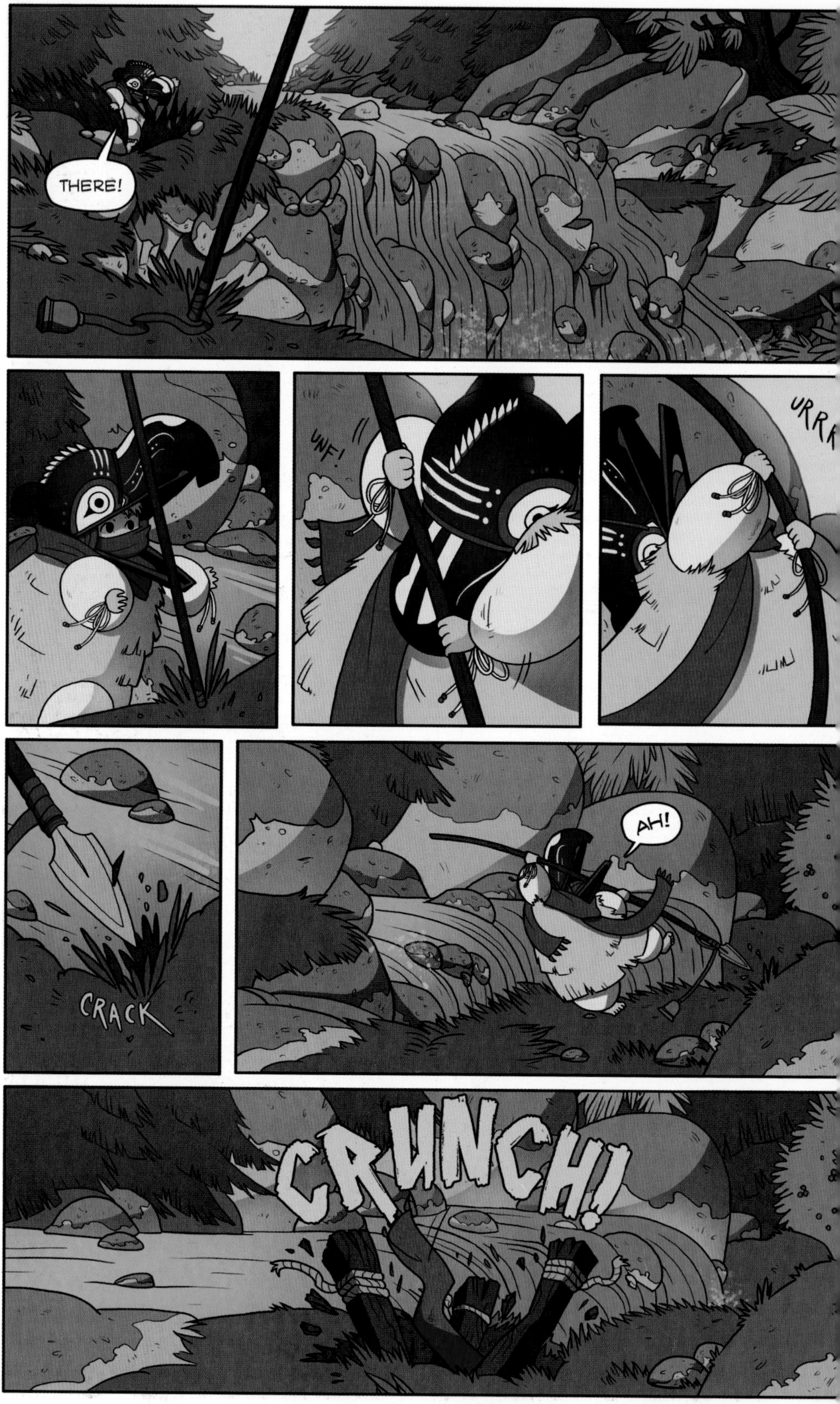
THERE!
UNF!
URRR
CRACK
AH!
CRUNCH!

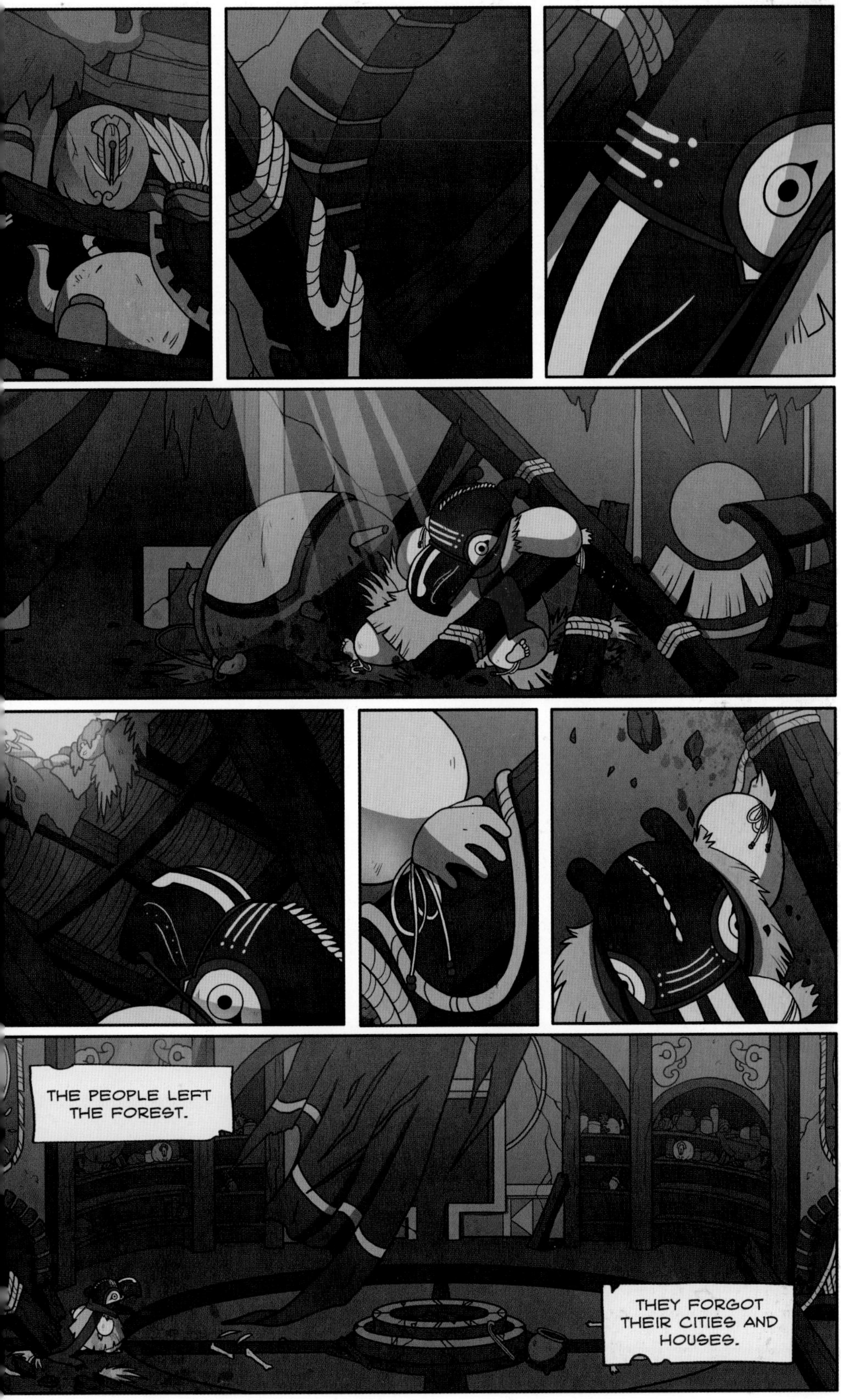
THE PEOPLE LEFT THE FOREST.
THEY FORGOT THEIR CITIES AND HOUSES.

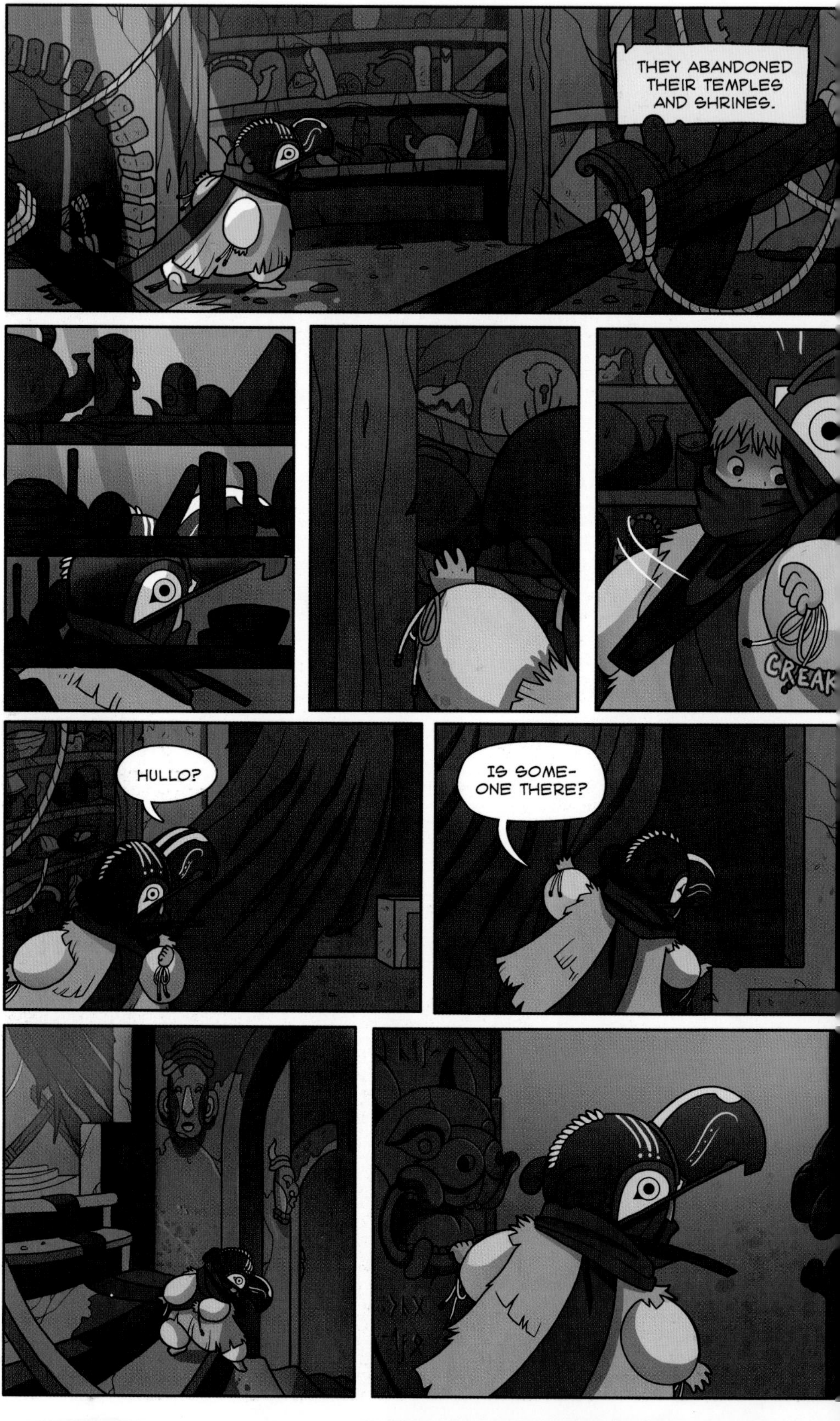
THEY ABANDONED THEIR TEMPLES AND SHRINES.
CREAK
HULLO?
IS SOME-ONE THERE?

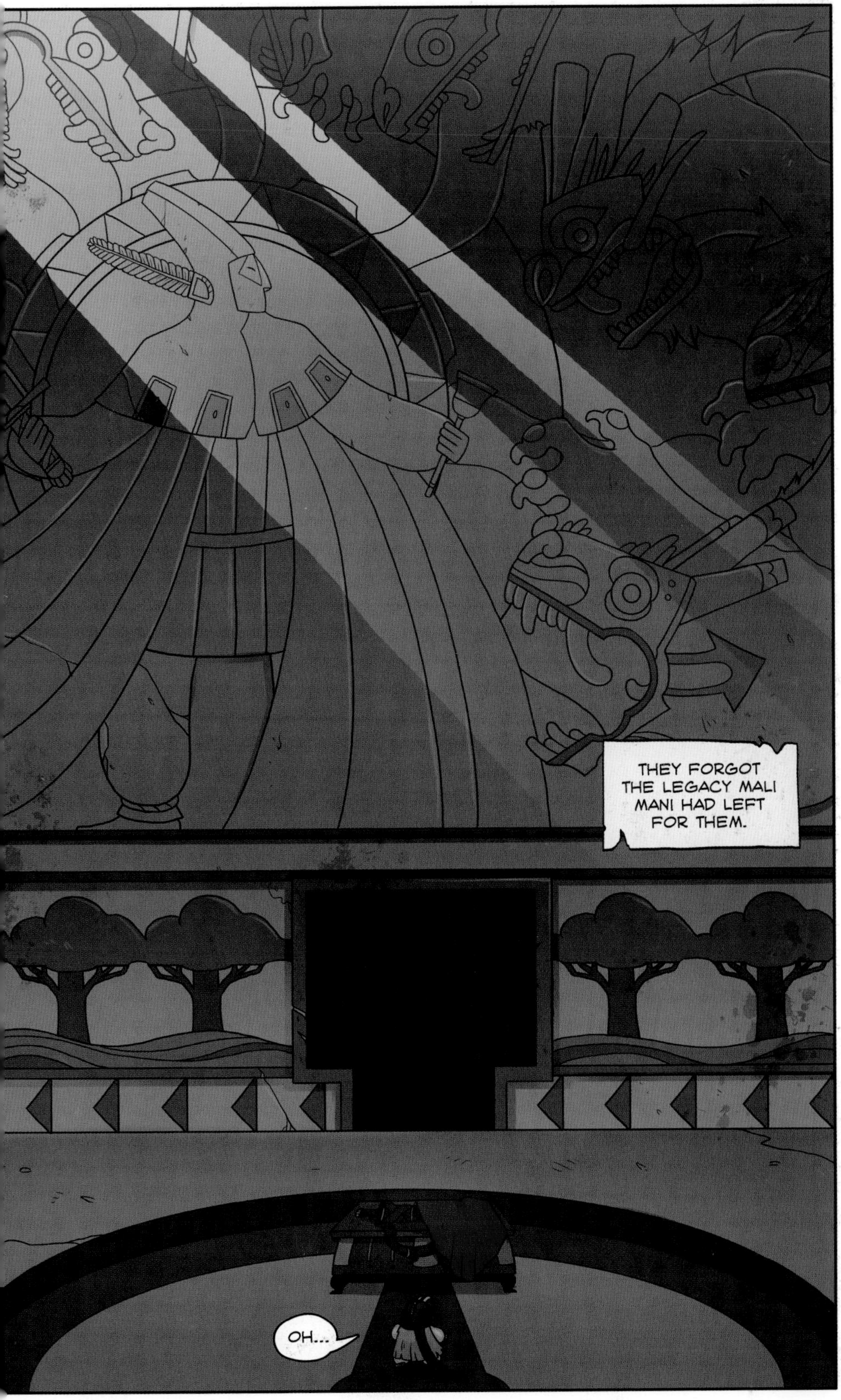
THEY FORGOT THE LEGACY MALI MANI HAD LEFT FOR THEM.
OH...

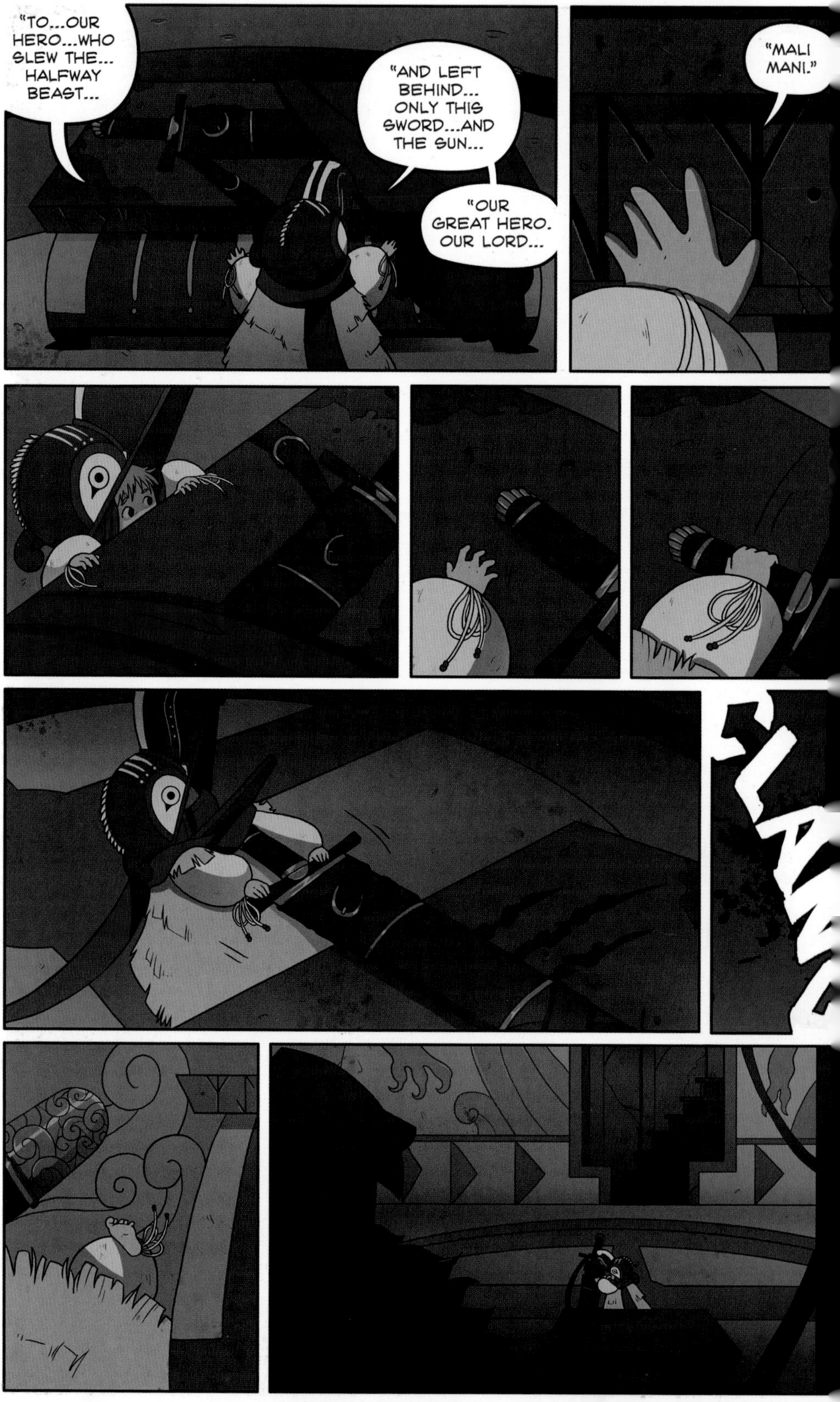
"TO...OUR HERO...WHO SLEW THE... HALFWAY BEAST...
"AND LEFT BEHIND... ONLY THIS SWORD...AND THE SUN...
"OUR GREAT HERO. OUR LORD...
"MALI MANI."

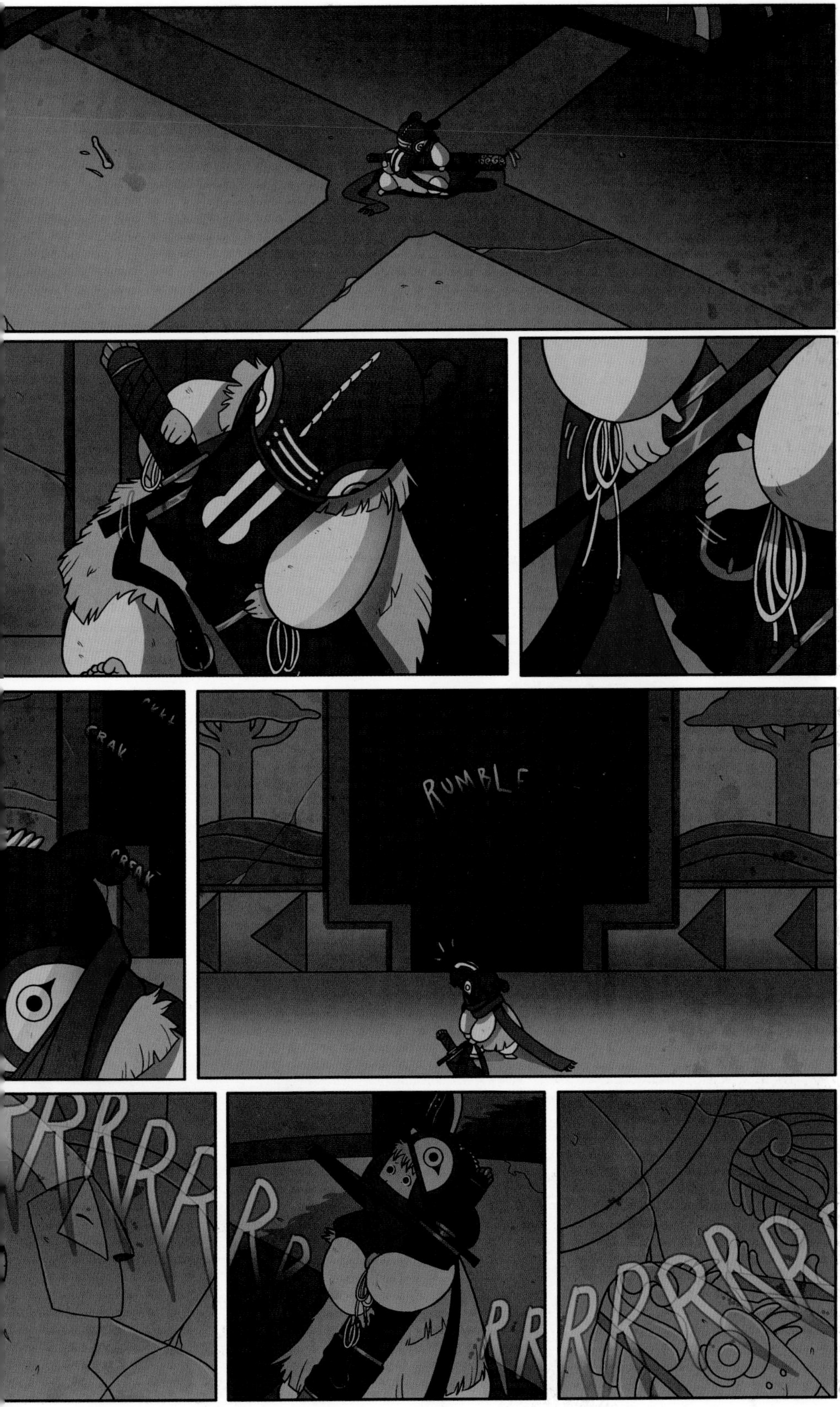
CRAK
CREAK
RUMBLE
RRRRRR
RR
RR
RRRRRRR

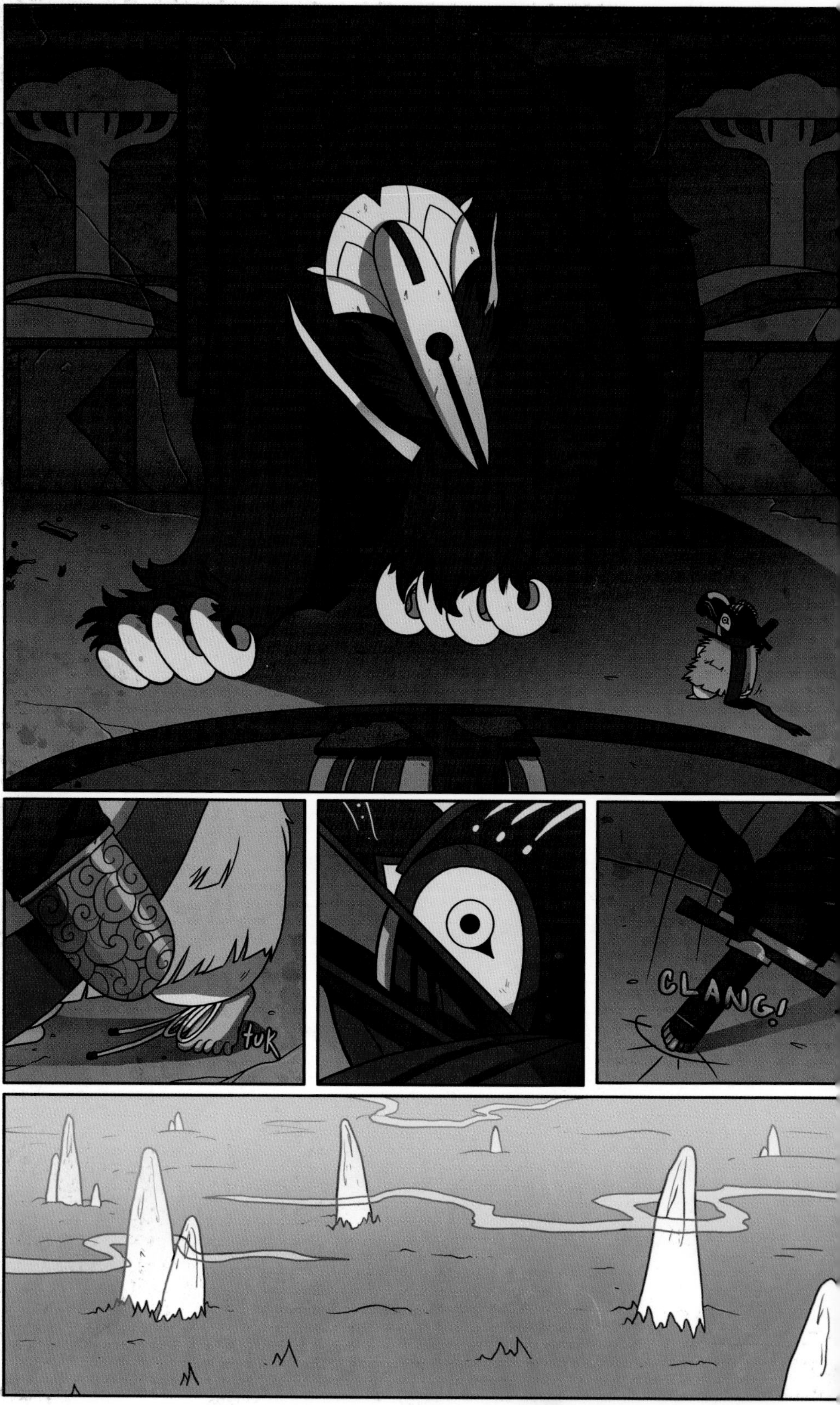
TUK
CLANG!

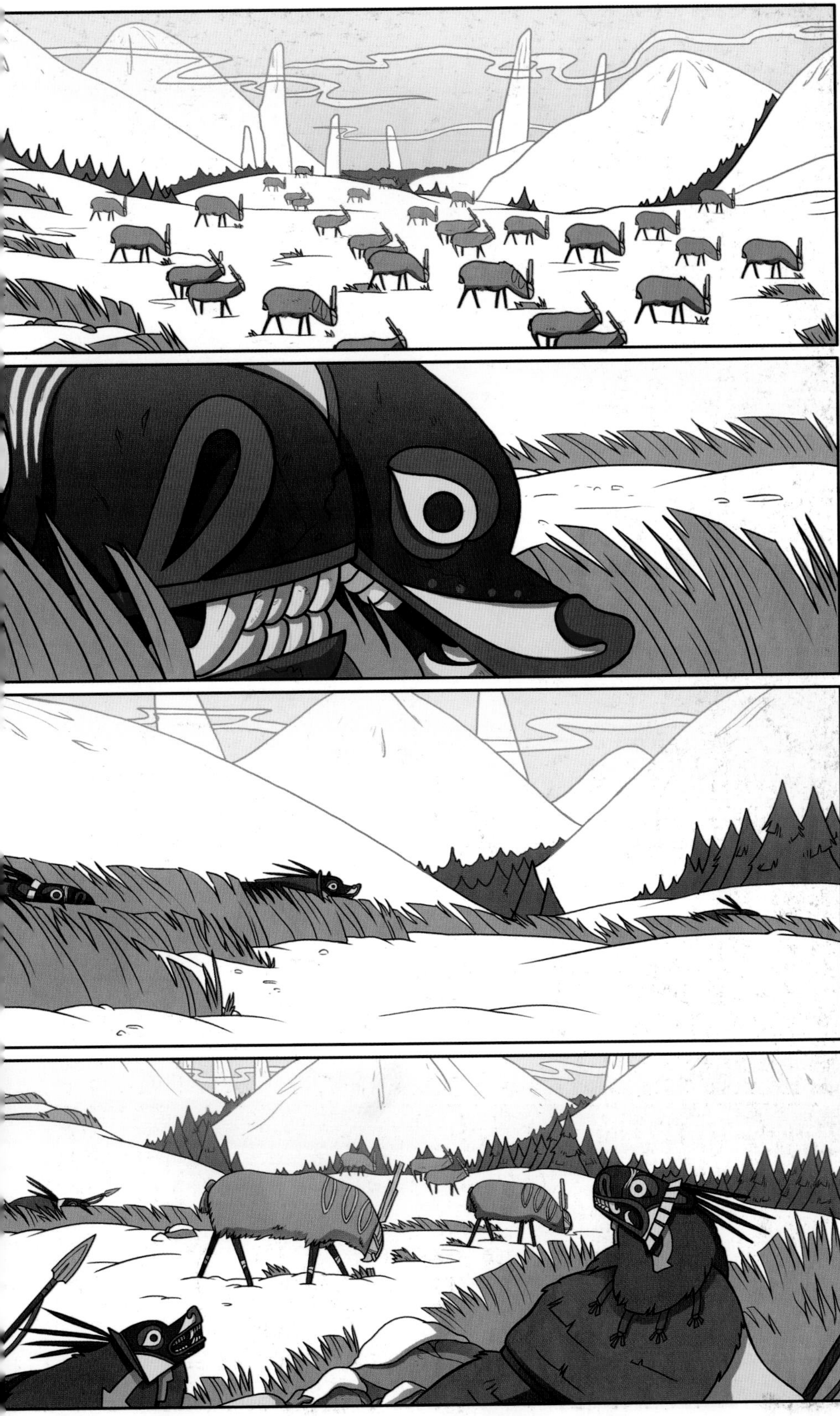

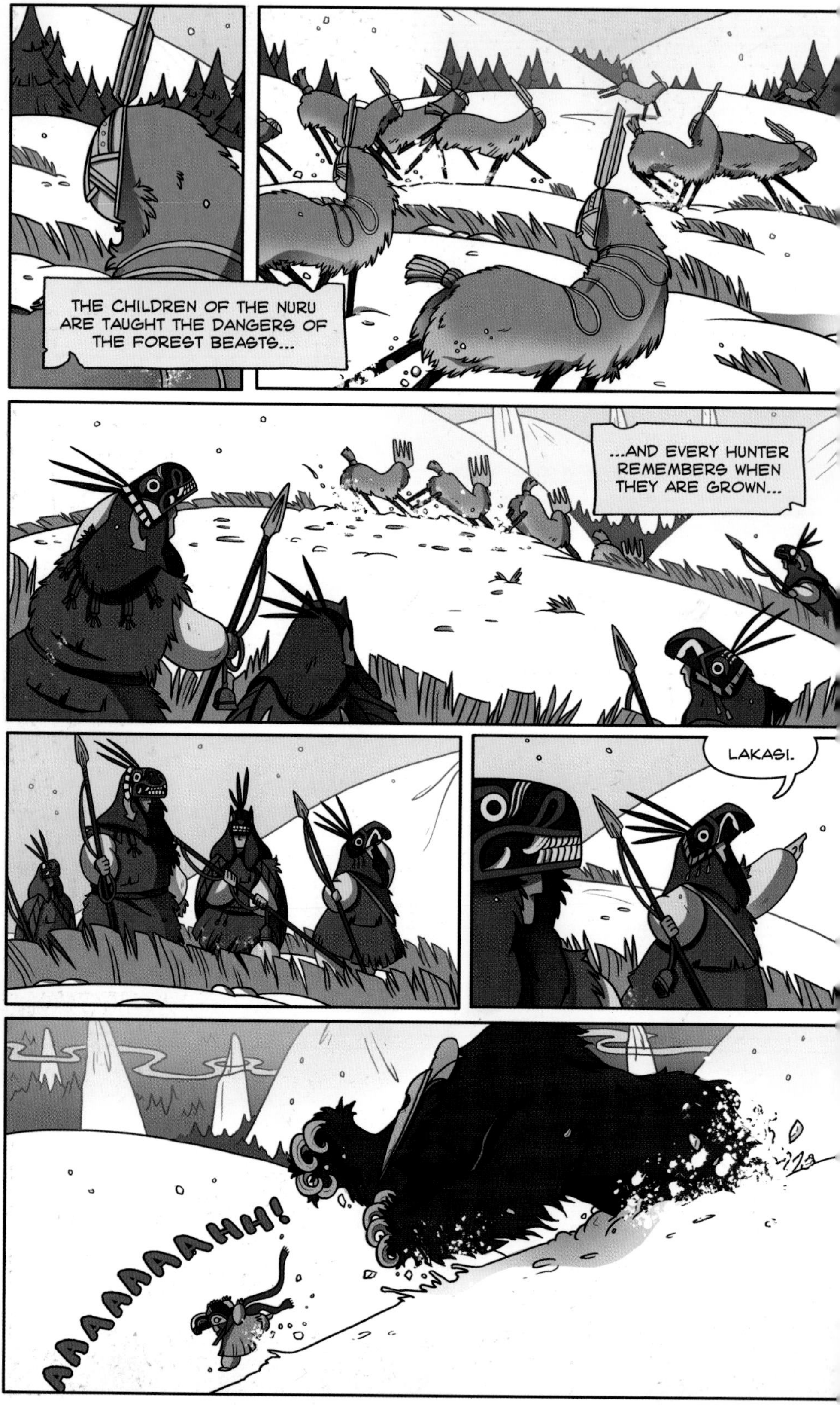
THE CHILDREN OF THE NURU ARE TAUGHT THE DANGERS OF THE FOREST BEASTS...
...AND EVERY HUNTER REMEMBERS WHEN THEY ARE GROWN...
LAKASI.
AAAAAAAAHH!

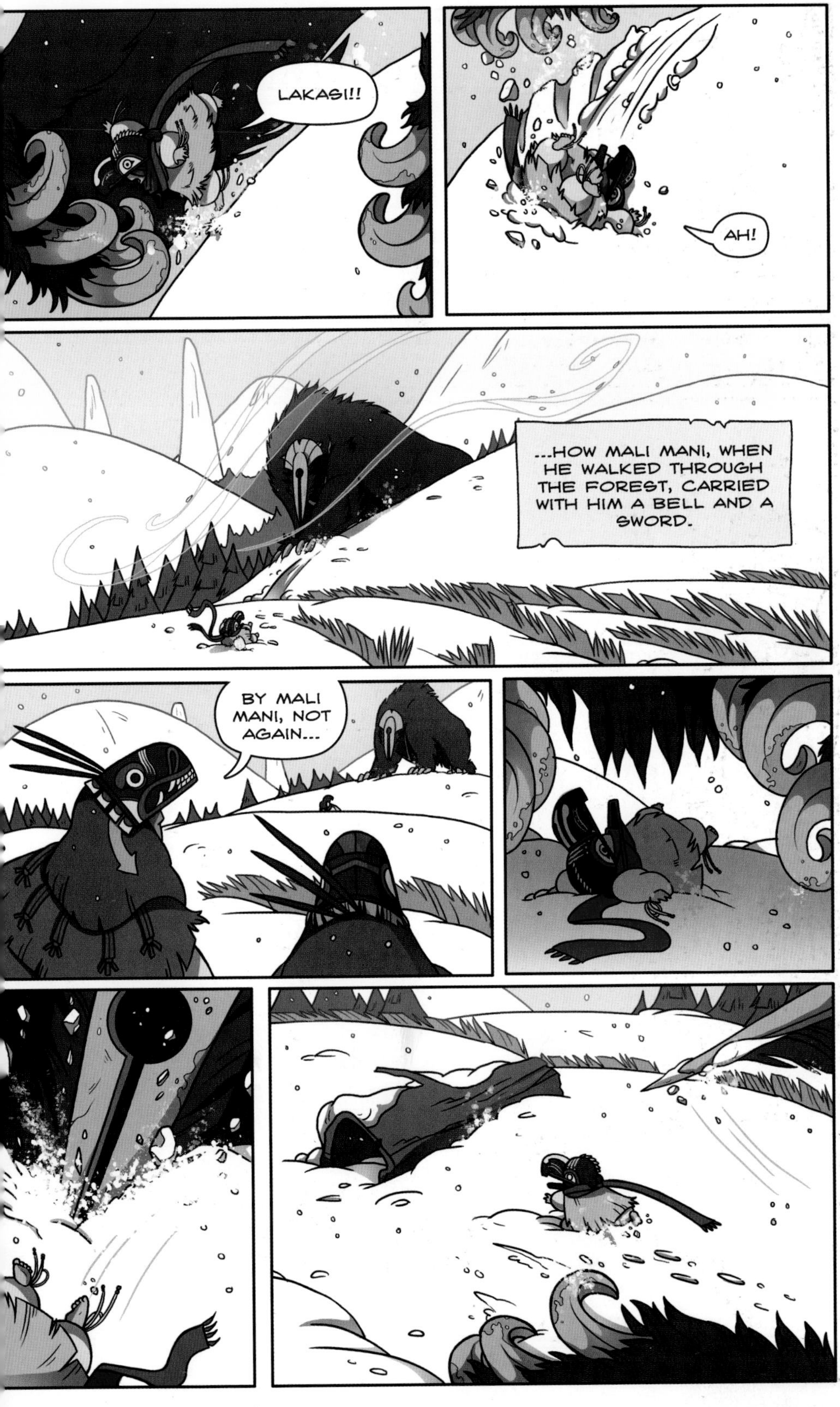
LAKASI!!
AH!
...HOW MALI MANI, WHEN HE WALKED THROUGH THE FOREST, CARRIED WITH HIM A BELL AND A SWORD.
BY MALI MANI, NOT AGAIN...

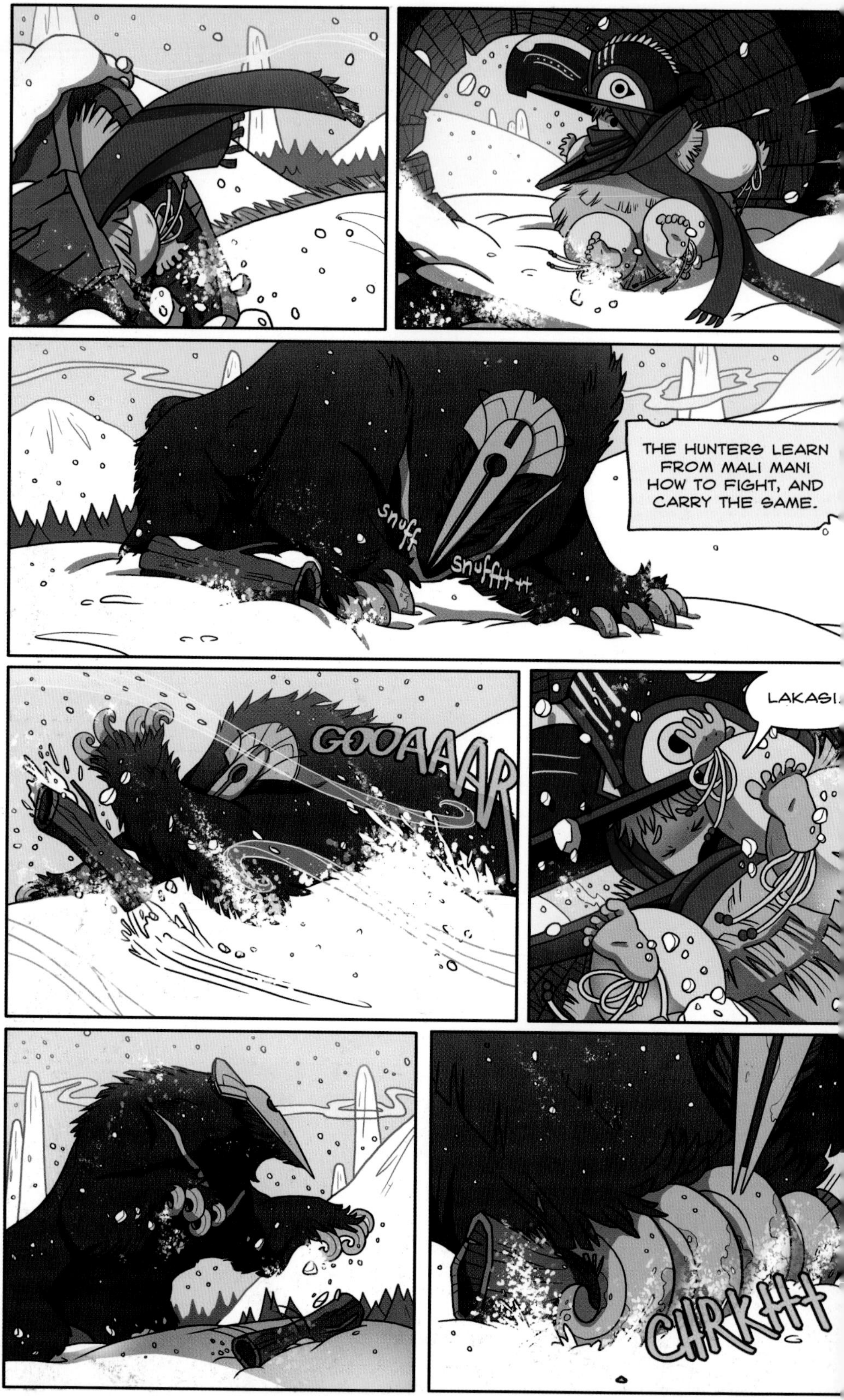
THE HUNTERS LEARN FROM MALI MANI HOW TO FIGHT, AND CARRY THE SAME.
snuff
snuffttt
GOOAAAAR
LAKASI.
CHRKTTT

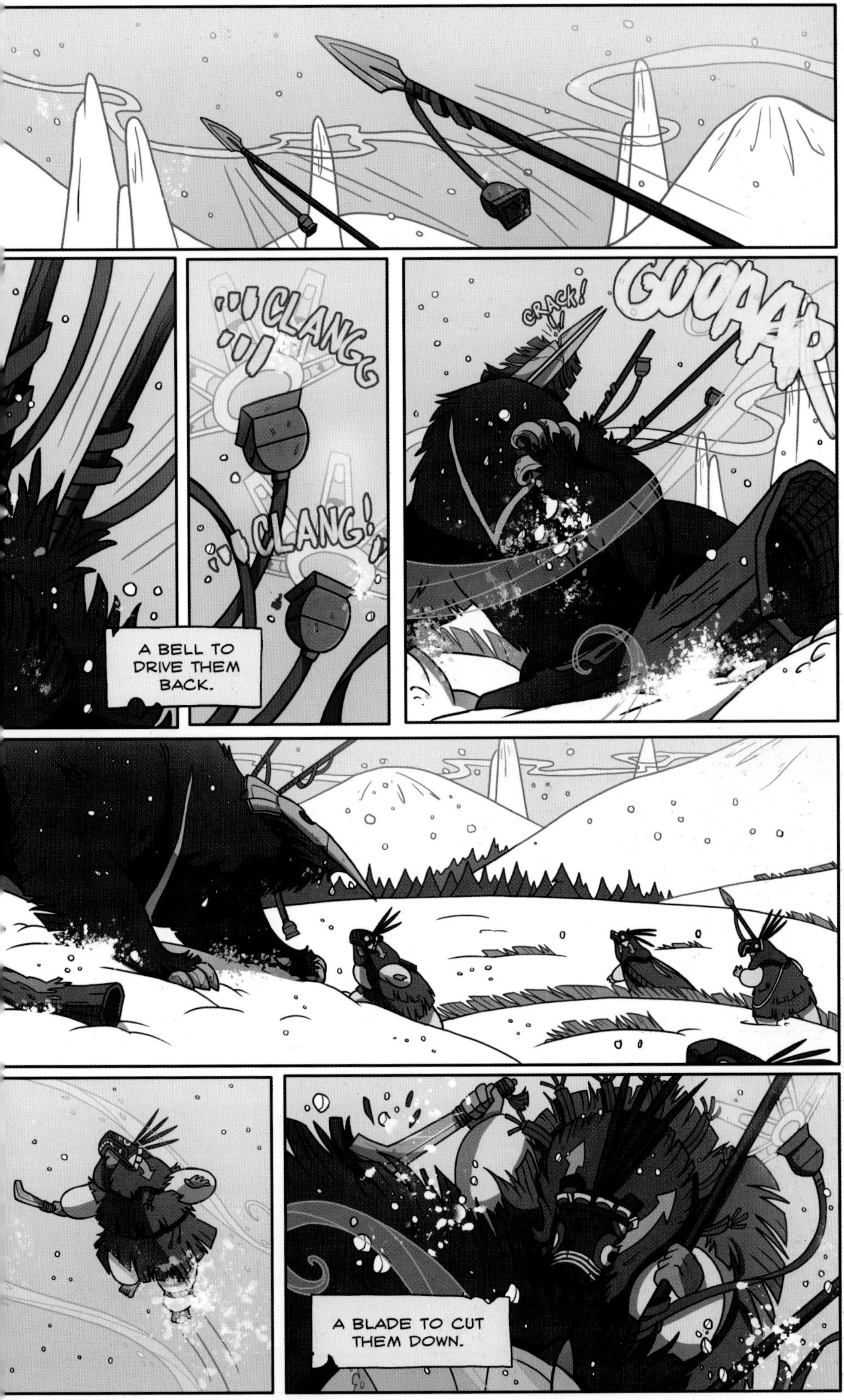

CLANGG
CLANG!
A BELL TO DRIVE THEM BACK.
CRACK!
GOOAAR
A BLADE TO CUT THEM DOWN.

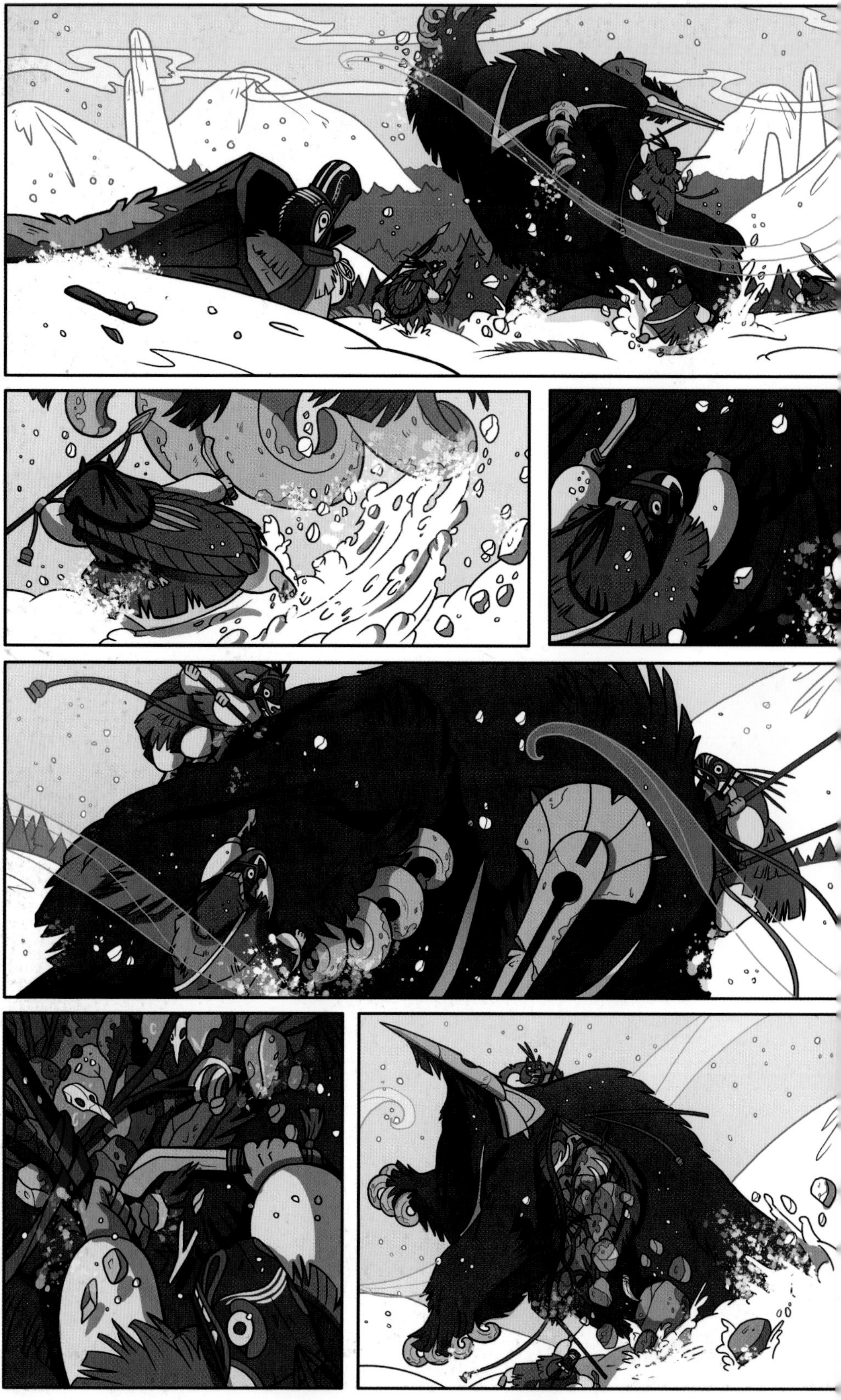

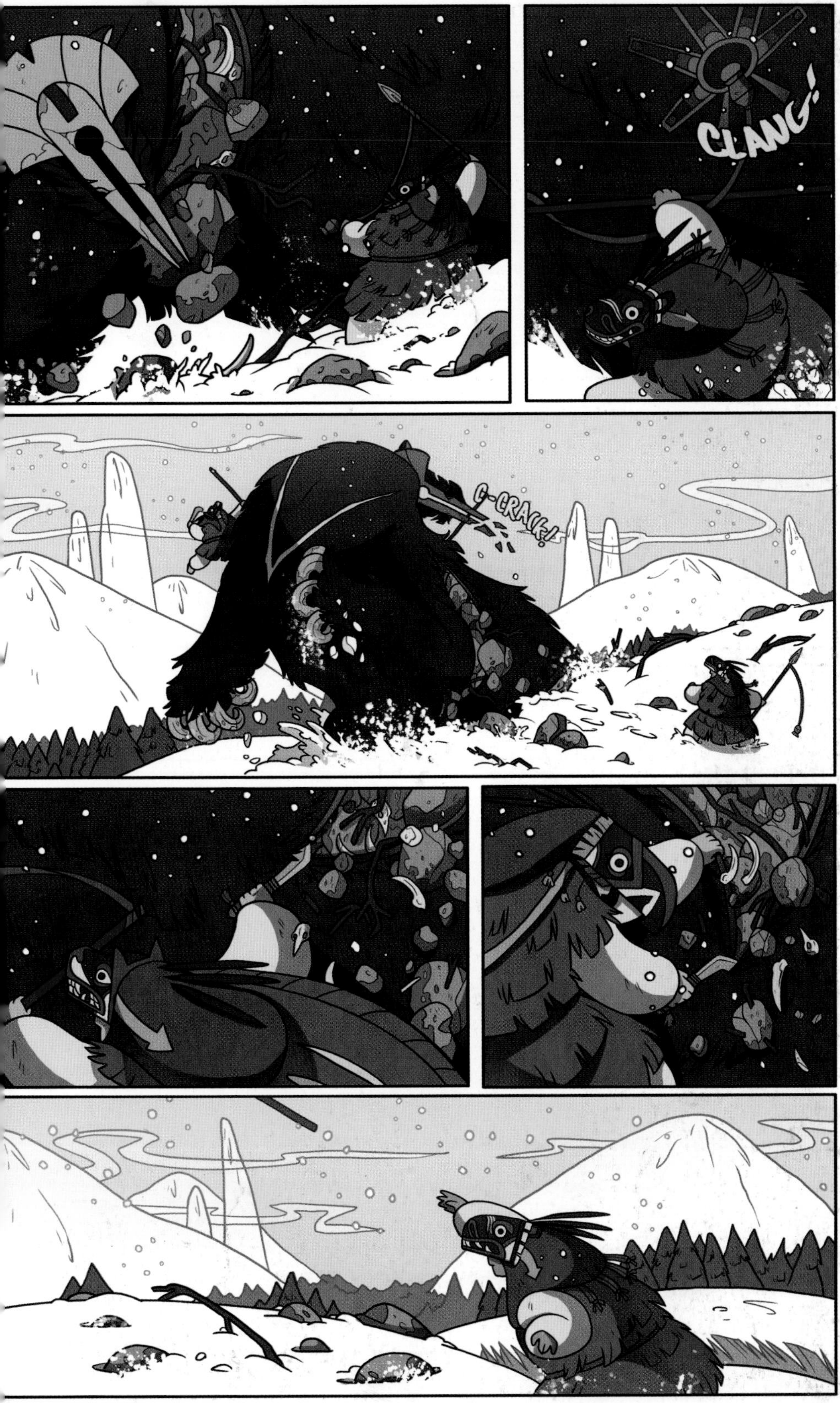
CLANG!
C-CRACK!

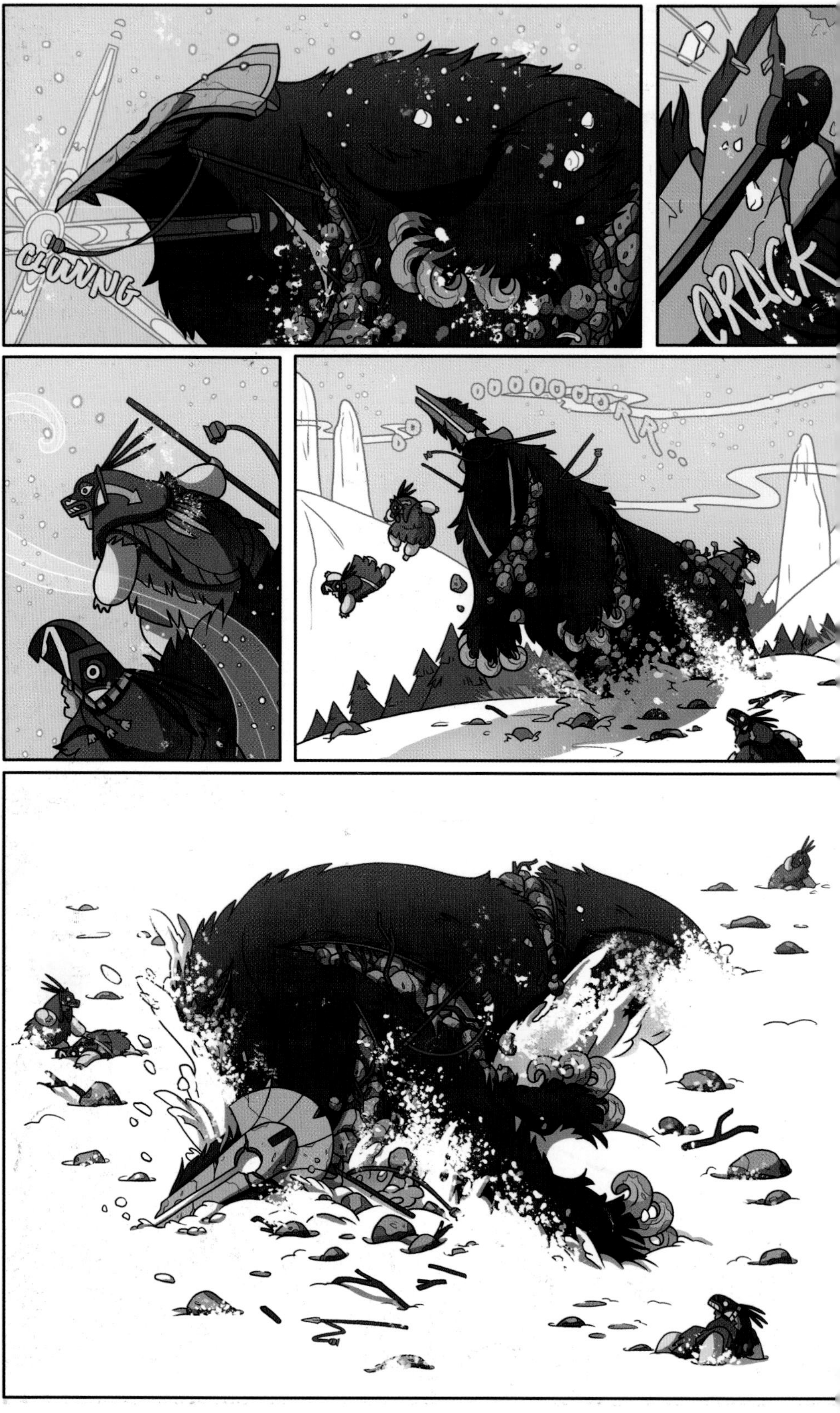
CLUNNG
CRACK
OOOOOOOORRR

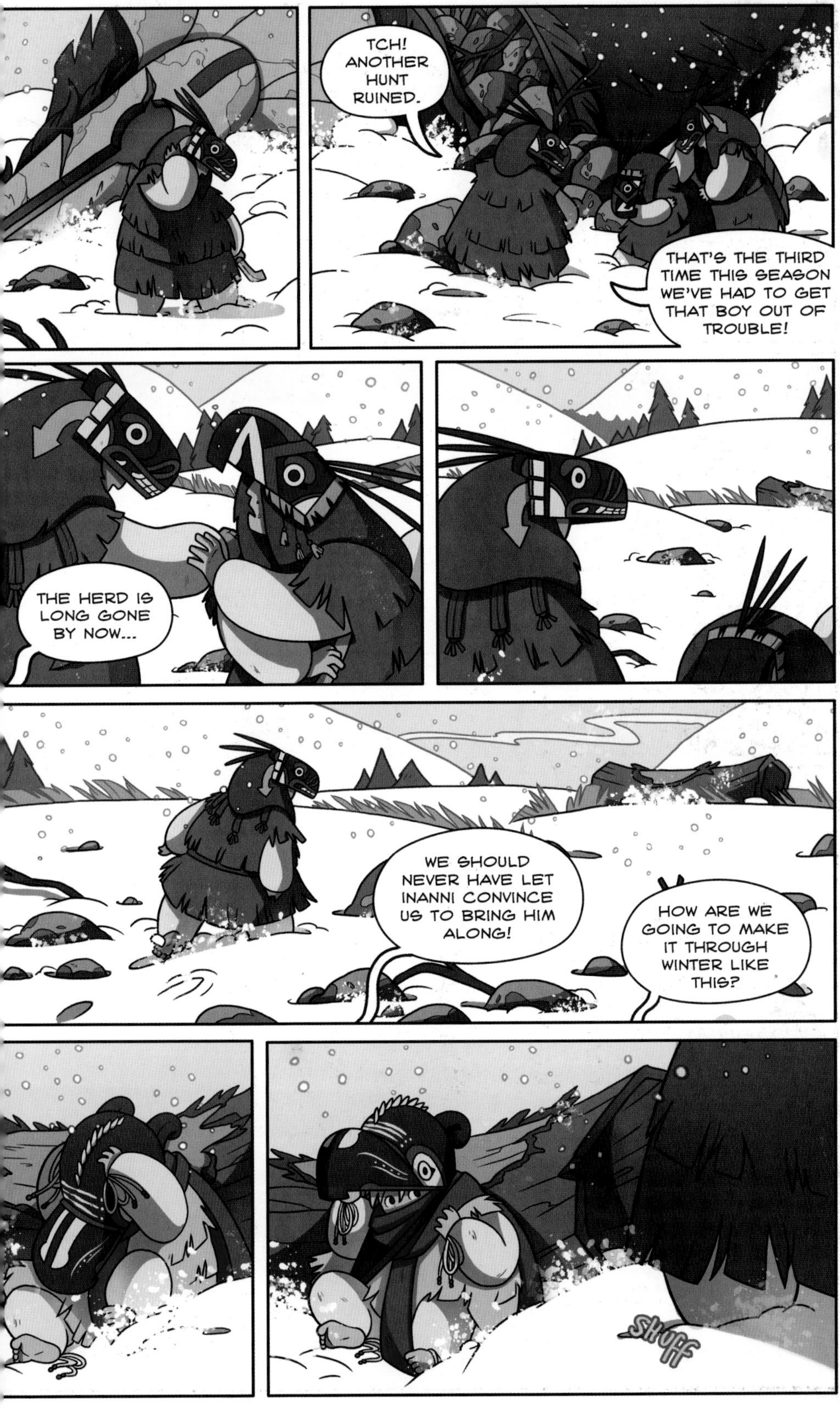
TCH! ANOTHER HUNT RUINED.
THAT'S THE THIRD TIME THIS SEASON WE'VE HAD TO GET THAT BOY OUT OF TROUBLE!
THE HERD IS LONG GONE BY NOW...
WE SHOULD NEVER HAVE LET INANNI CONVINCE US TO BRING HIM ALONG!
HOW ARE WE GOING TO MAKE IT THROUGH WINTER LIKE THIS?
SHUFF

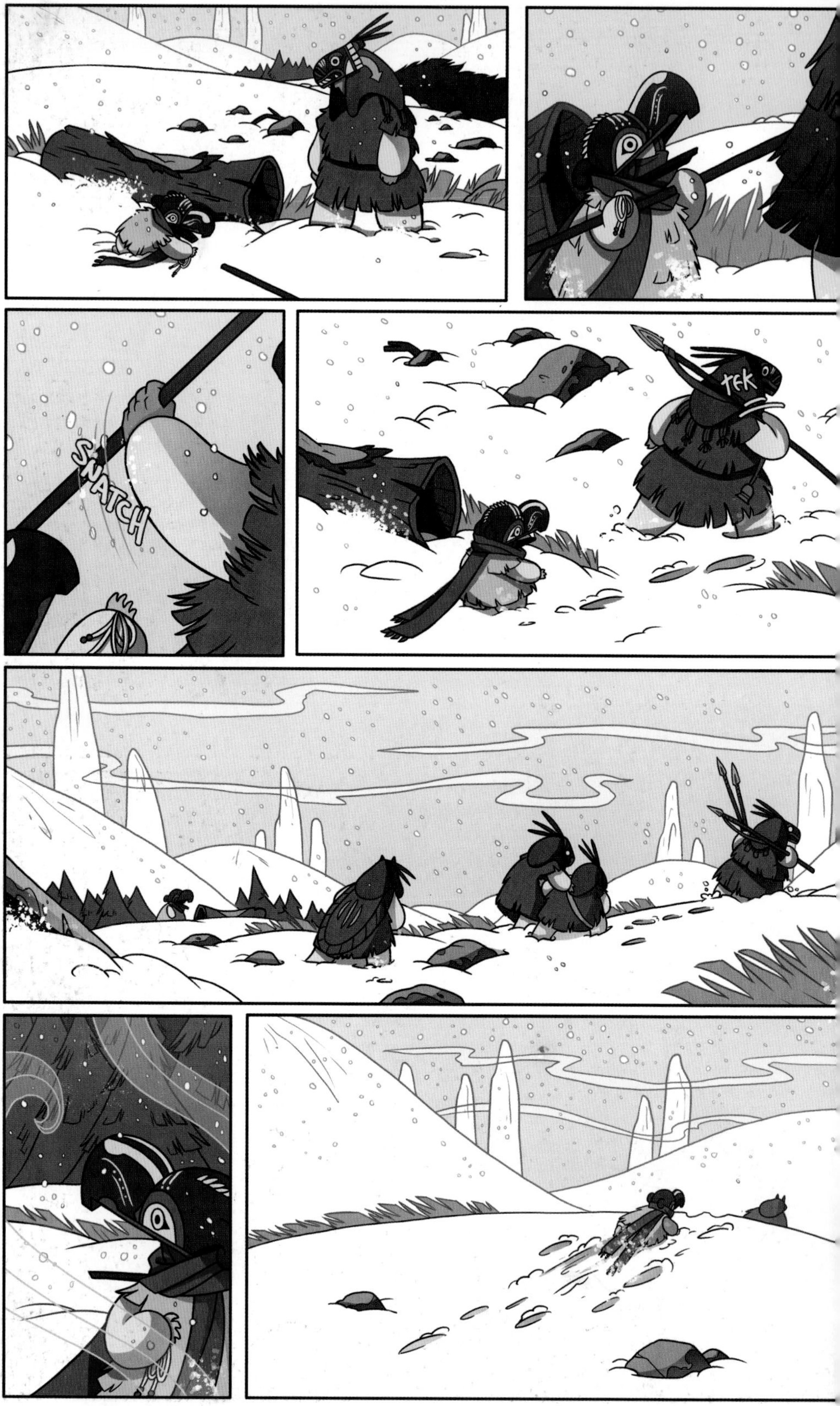
SNATCH
TEK

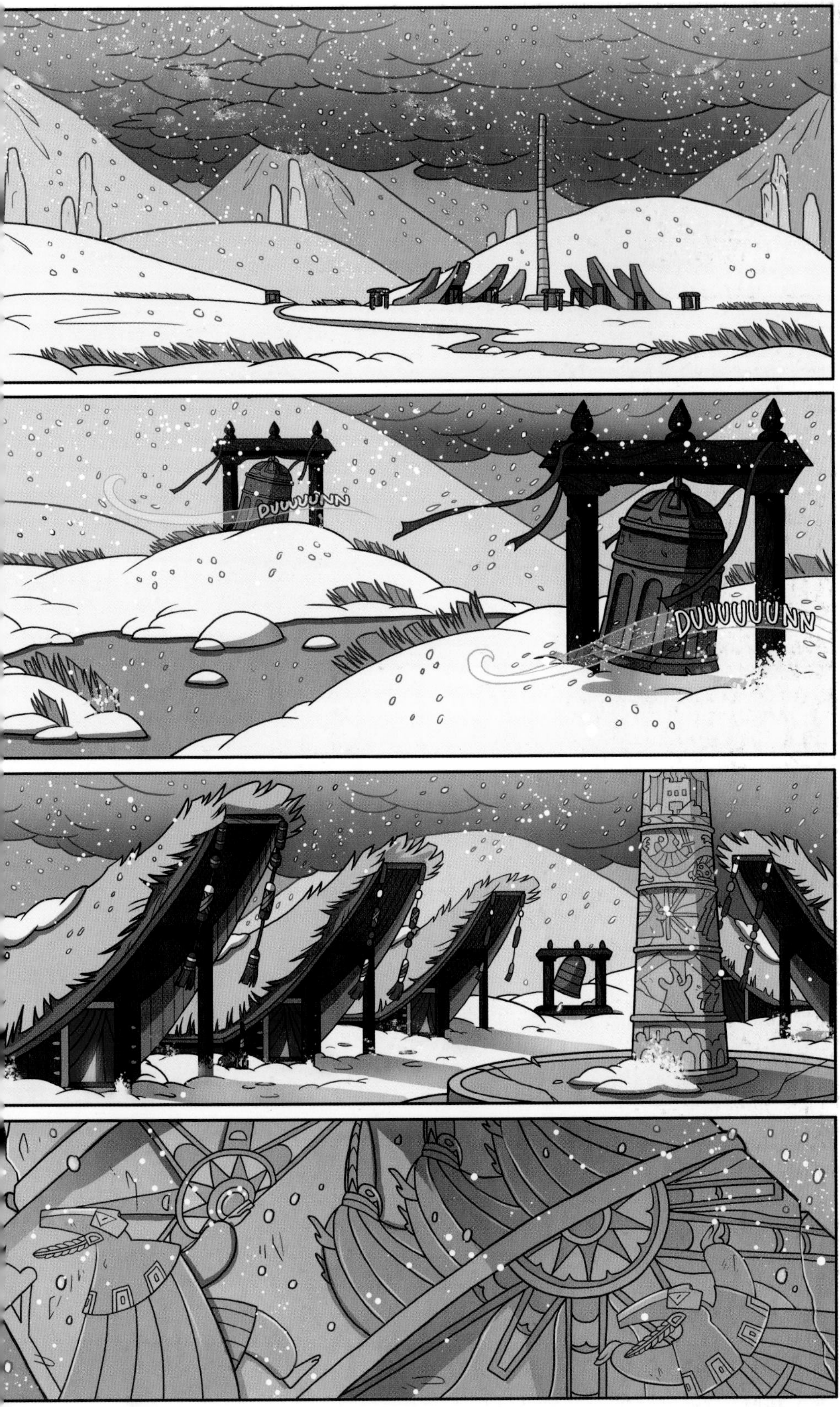
DUUUUNN
DUUUUUUNN

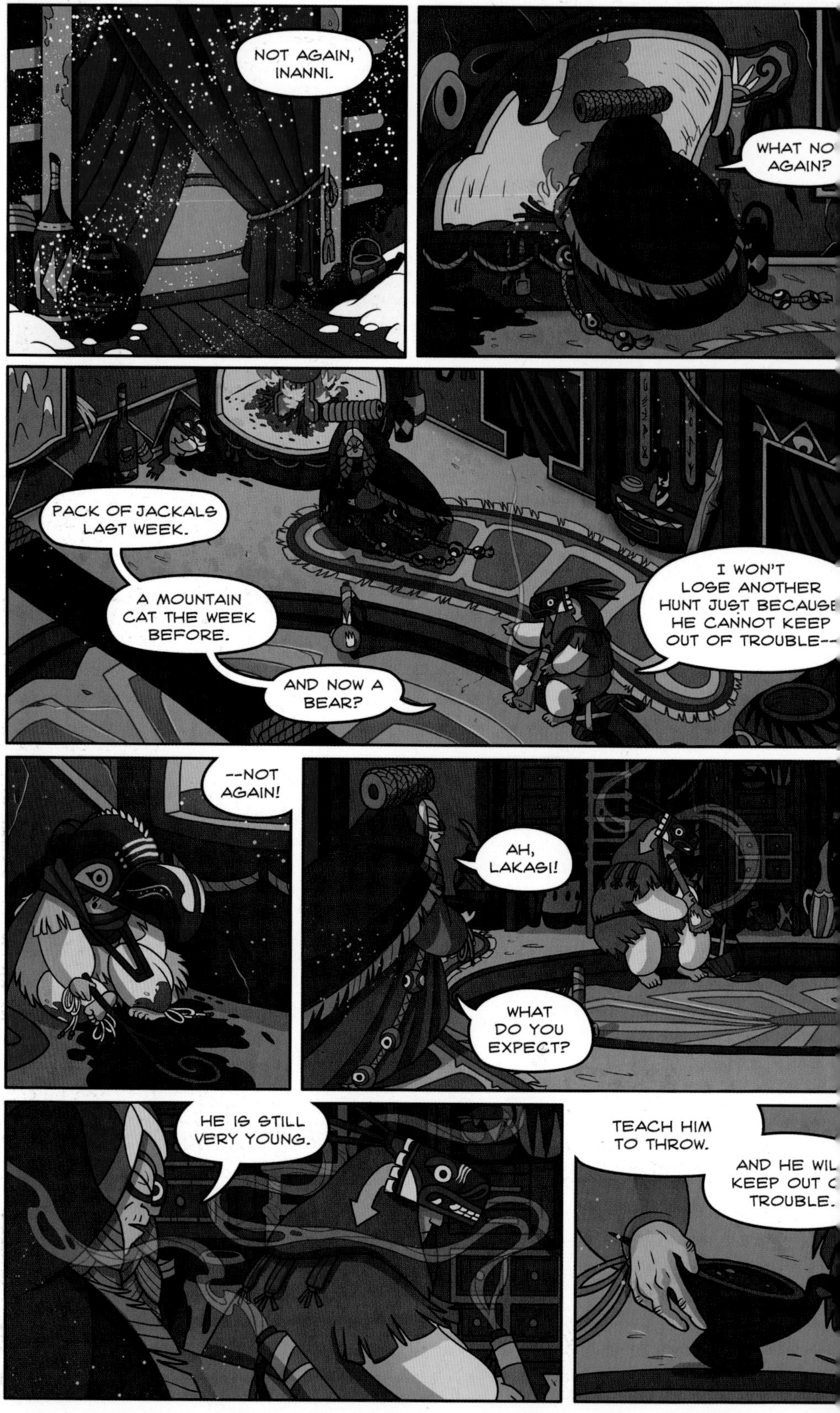
NOT AGAIN, INANNI.
WHAT NO AGAIN?
PACK OF JACKALS LAST WEEK.
A MOUNTAIN CAT THE WEEK BEFORE.
AND NOW A BEAR?
I WON'T LOSE ANOTHER HUNT JUST BECAUSE HE CANNOT KEEP OUT OF TROUBLE--
--NOT AGAIN!
AH, LAKASI!
WHAT DO YOU EXPECT?
HE IS STILL VERY YOUNG.
TEACH HIM TO THROW.
AND HE WIL KEEP OUT O TROUBLE.

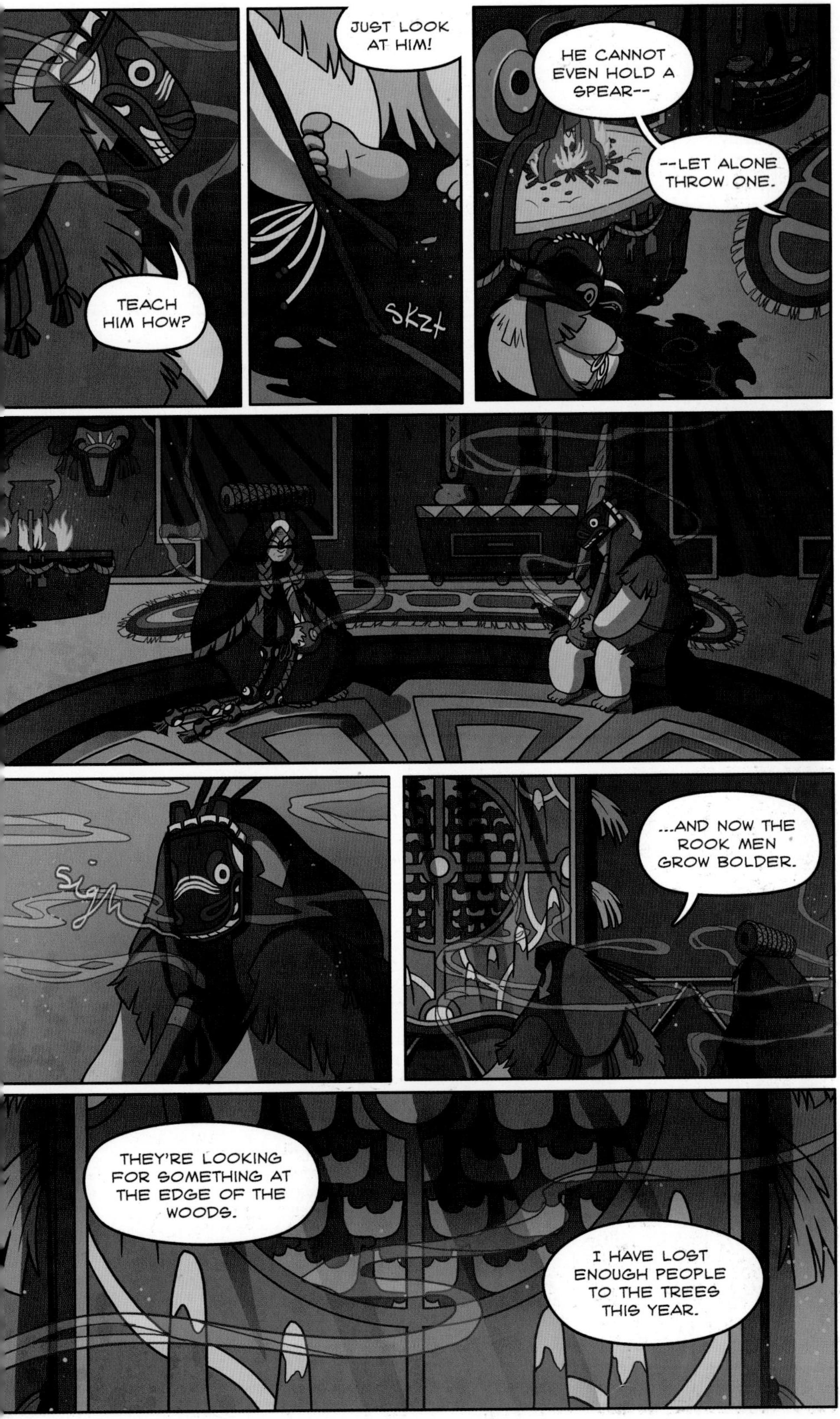
TEACH HIM HOW?
JUST LOOK AT HIM!
SKZT
HE CANNOT EVEN HOLD A SPEAR--
--LET ALONE THROW ONE.
SIGH
...AND NOW THE ROOK MEN GROW BOLDER.
THEY'RE LOOKING FOR SOMETHING AT THE EDGE OF THE WOODS.
I HAVE LOST ENOUGH PEOPLE TO THE TREES THIS YEAR.

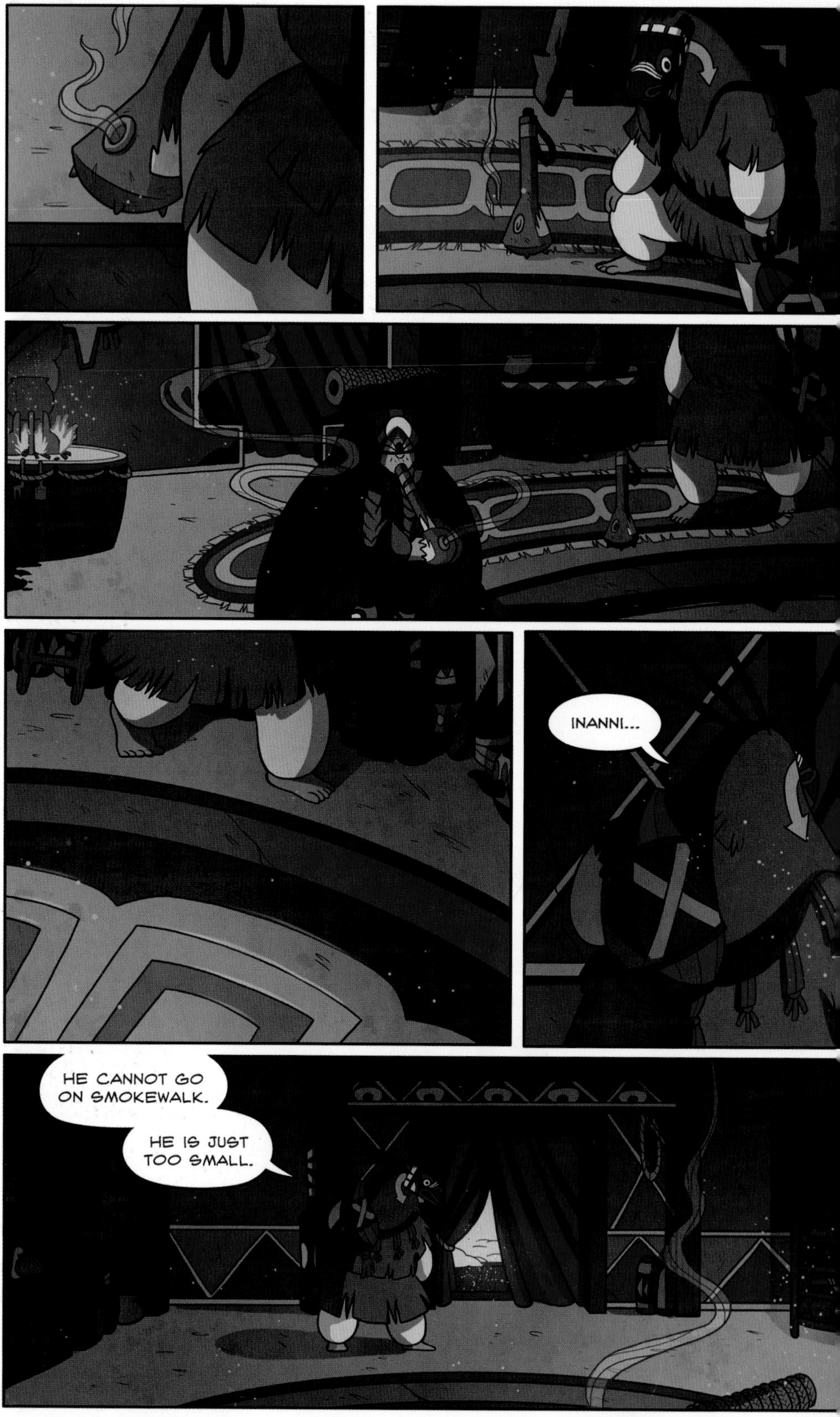
INANNI...
HE CANNOT GO ON SMOKEWALK.
HE IS JUST TOO SMALL.

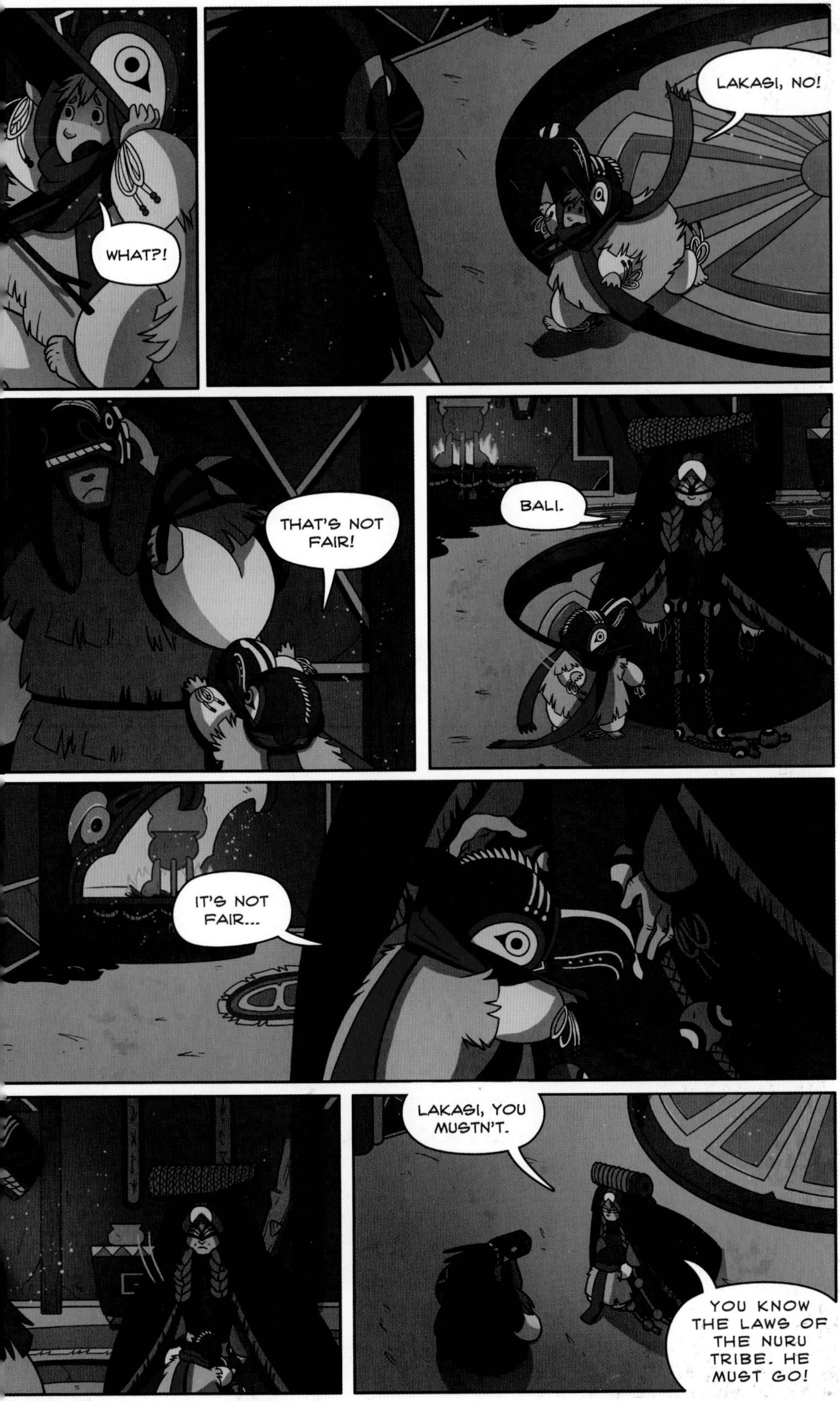
WHAT?!
LAKASI, NO!
THAT'S NOT FAIR!
BALI.
IT'S NOT FAIR...
LAKASI, YOU MUSTN'T.
YOU KNOW THE LAWS OF THE NURU TRIBE. HE MUST GO!

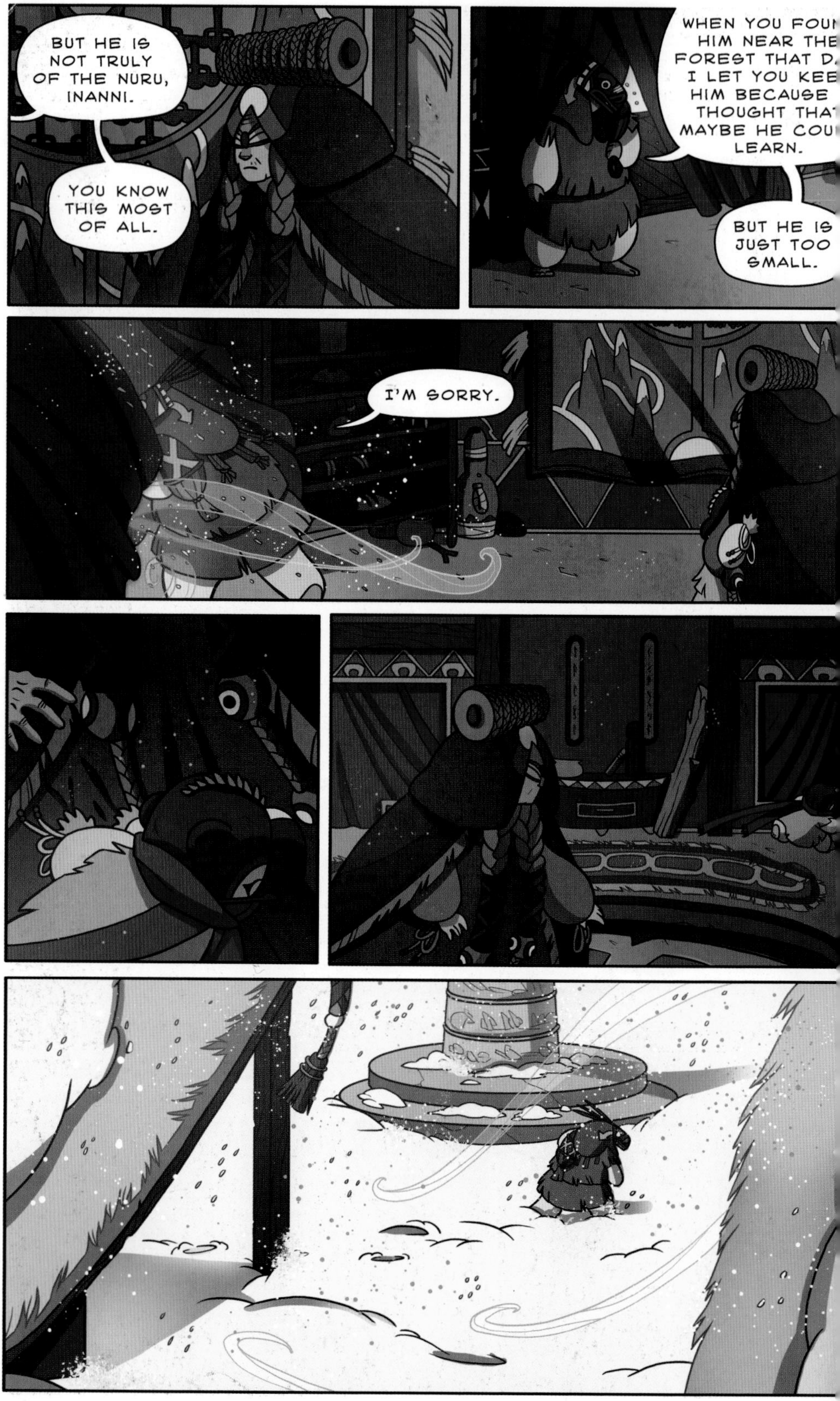
BUT HE IS NOT TRULY OF THE NURU, INANNI.
YOU KNOW THIS MOST OF ALL.
WHEN YOU FOU HIM NEAR THE FOREST THAT D I LET YOU KEE HIM BECAUSE THOUGHT THA MAYBE HE COU LEARN.
BUT HE IS JUST TOO SMALL.
I'M SORRY.

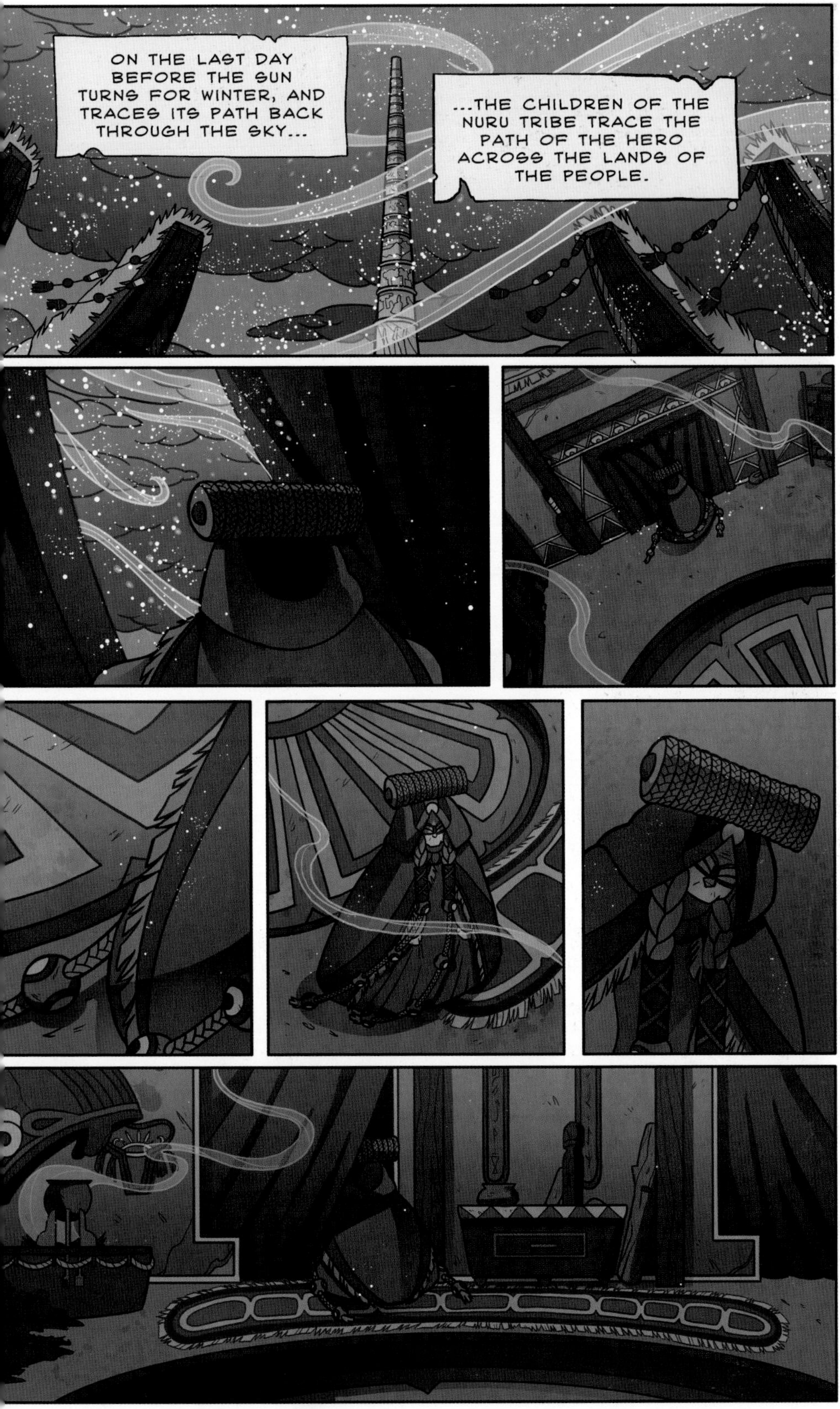
ON THE LAST DAY BEFORE THE SUN TURNS FOR WINTER, AND TRACES ITS PATH BACK THROUGH THE SKY...
...THE CHILDREN OF THE NURU TRIBE TRACE THE PATH OF THE HERO ACROSS THE LANDS OF THE PEOPLE.

IT IS CALLED A SMOKEWALK.

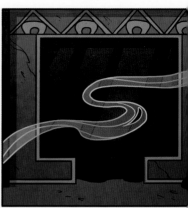

SNIF.

FOR WHEN MALI MANI MADE HIS WAY THROUGH THE FOREST TO FACE THE HALFWAY BEAST...

...HE TRAVELED THROUGH A DARKNESS AS THICK AND HEAVY AS SMOKE.

SNUFF.

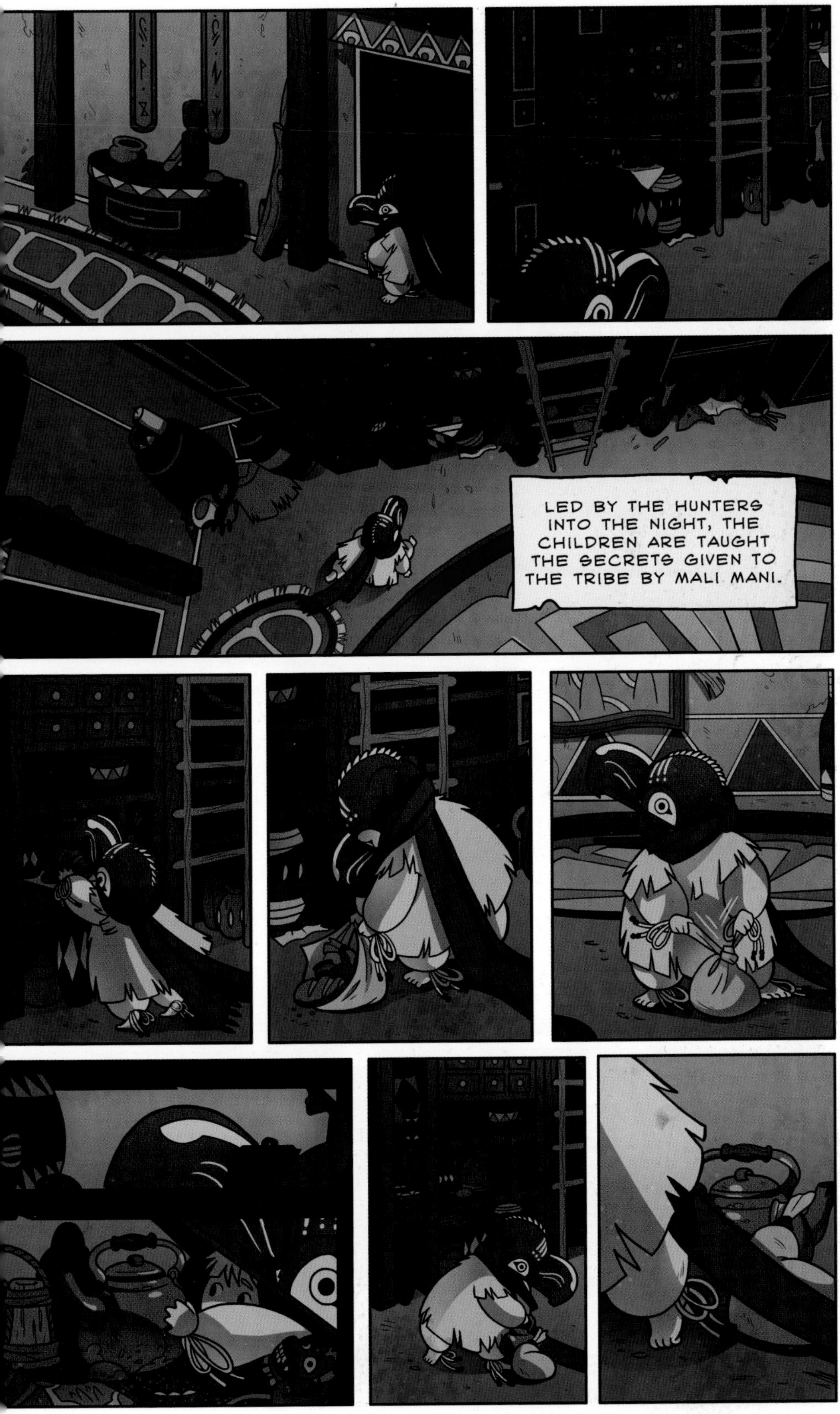
LED BY THE HUNTERS INTO THE NIGHT, THE CHILDREN ARE TAUGHT THE SECRETS GIVEN TO THE TRIBE BY MALI MANI.

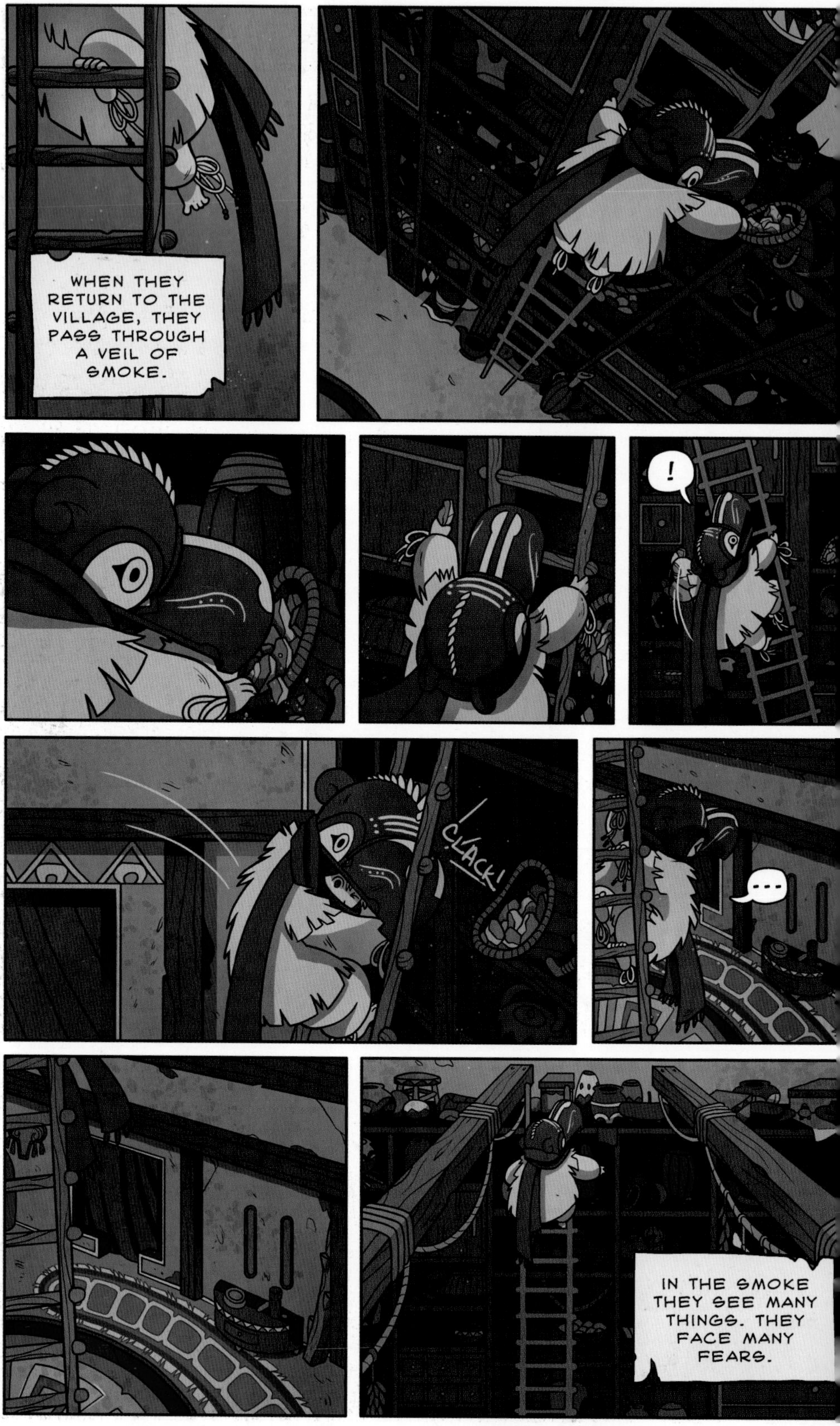
WHEN THEY RETURN TO THE VILLAGE, THEY PASS THROUGH A VEIL OF SMOKE.
!
CLACK!
...
IN THE SMOKE THEY SEE MANY THINGS. THEY FACE MANY FEARS.

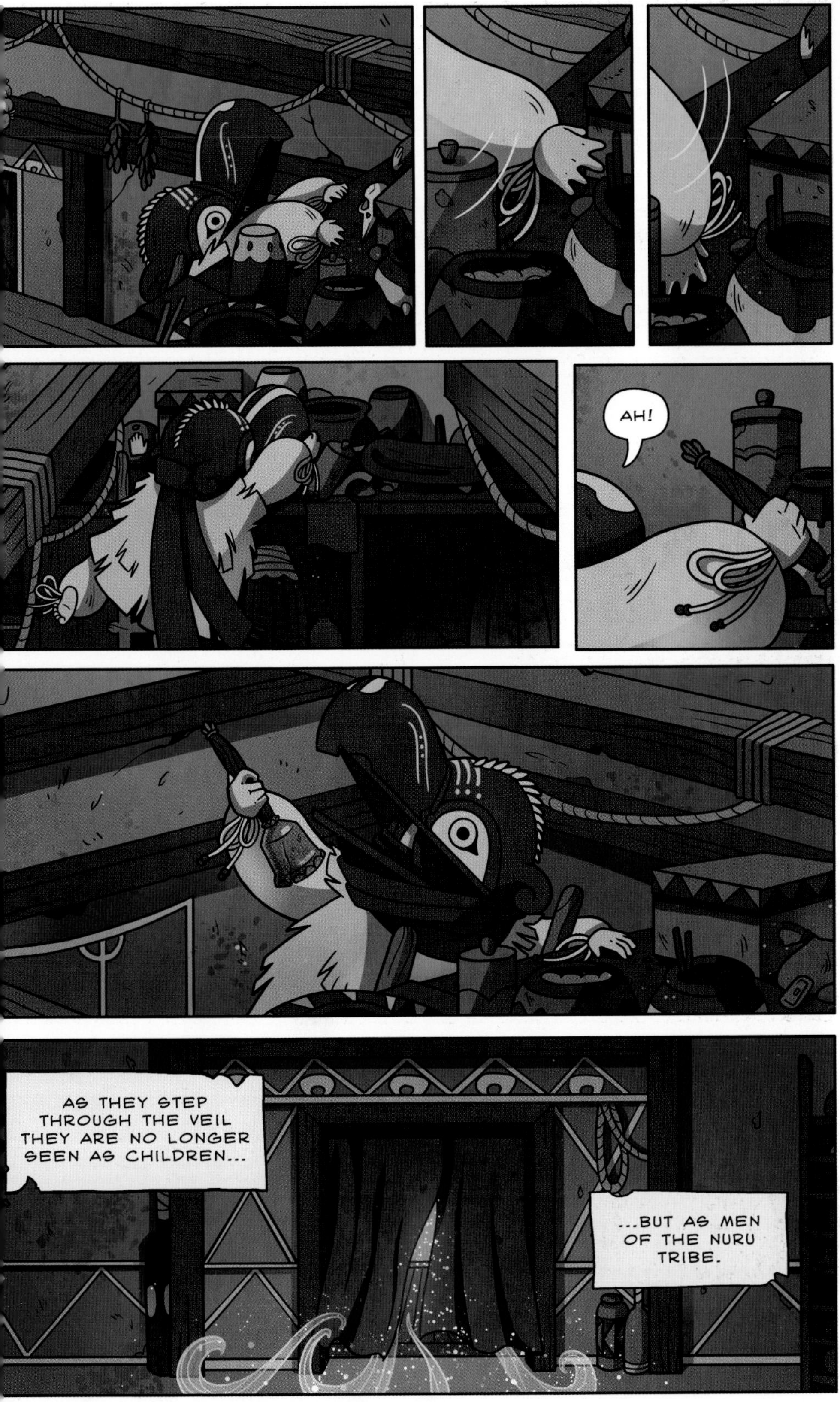
AH!
AS THEY STEP THROUGH THE VEIL THEY ARE NO LONGER SEEN AS CHILDREN...
...BUT AS MEN OF THE NURU TRIBE.

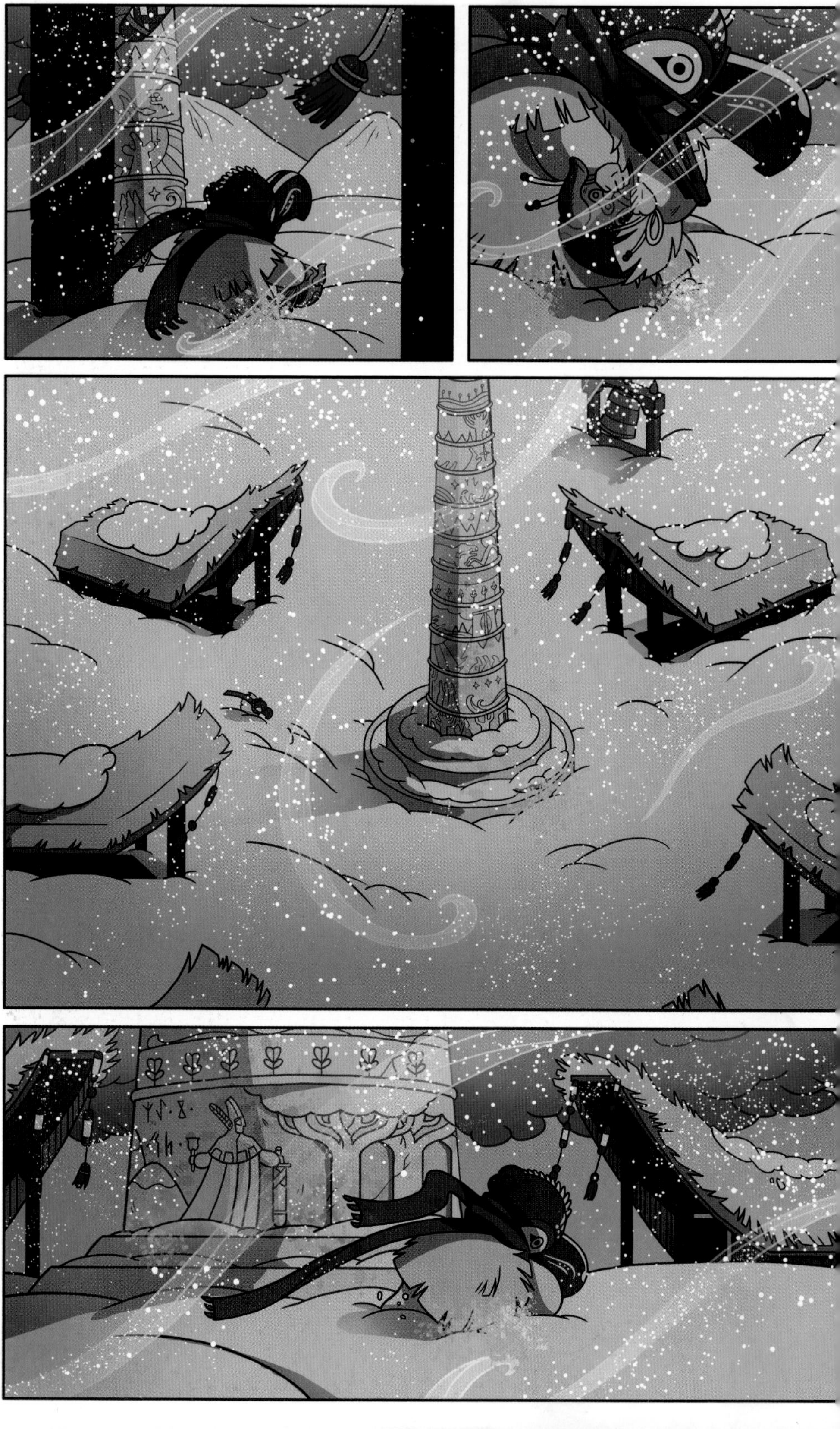

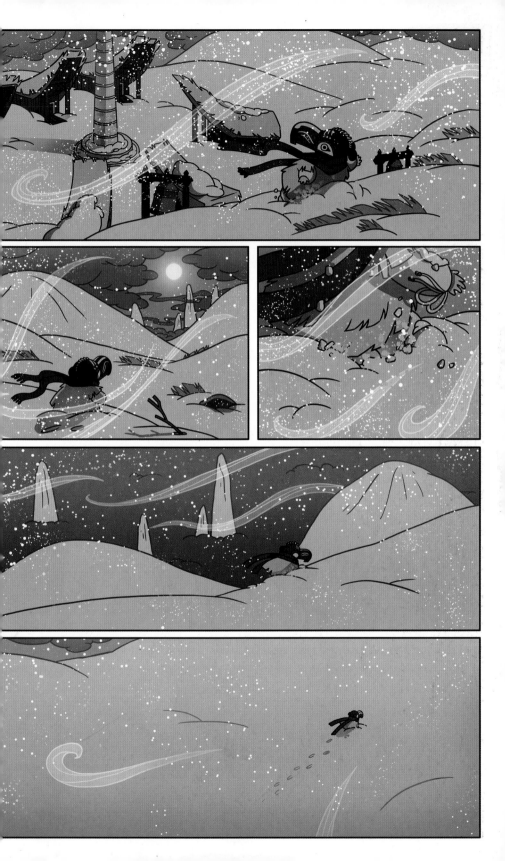

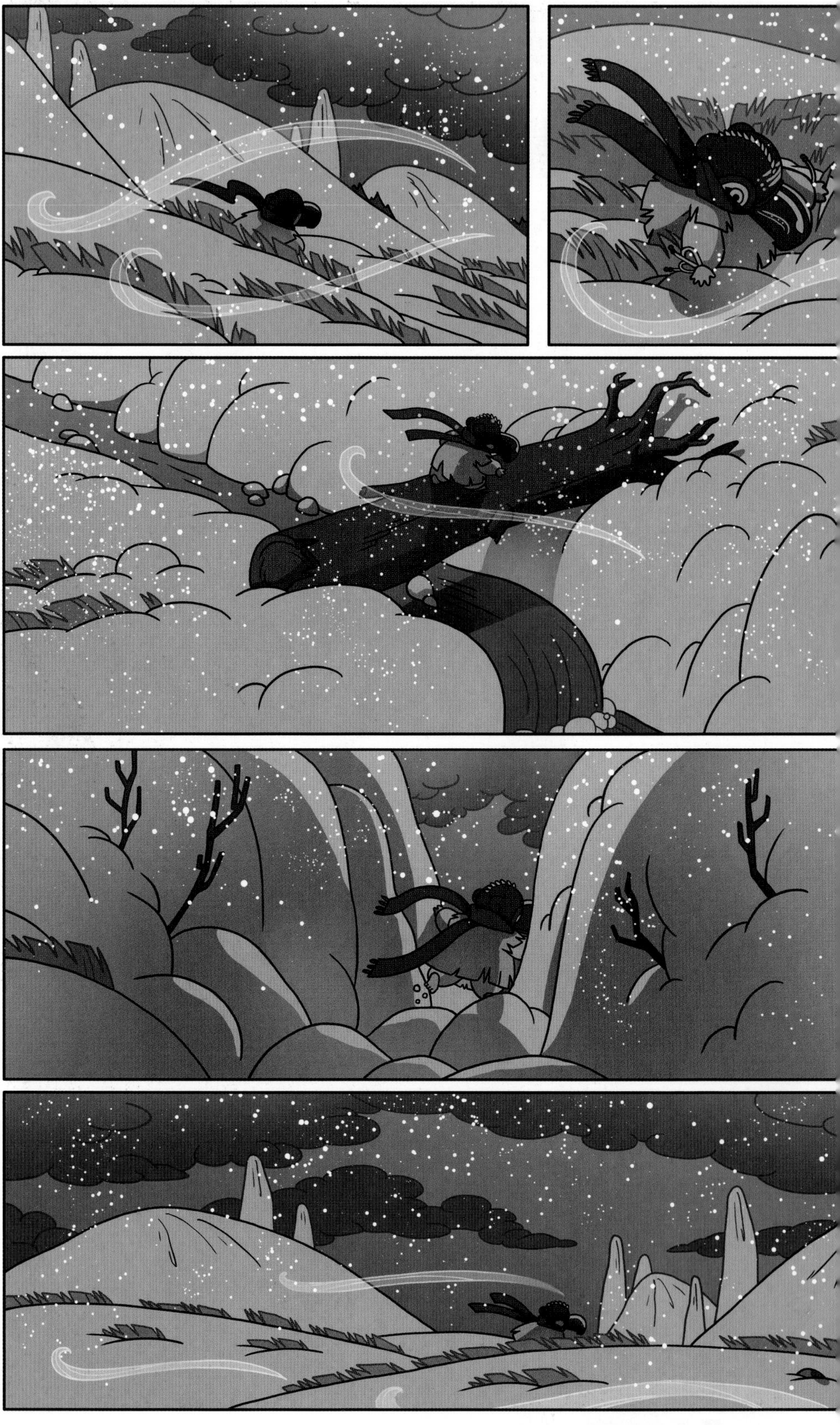

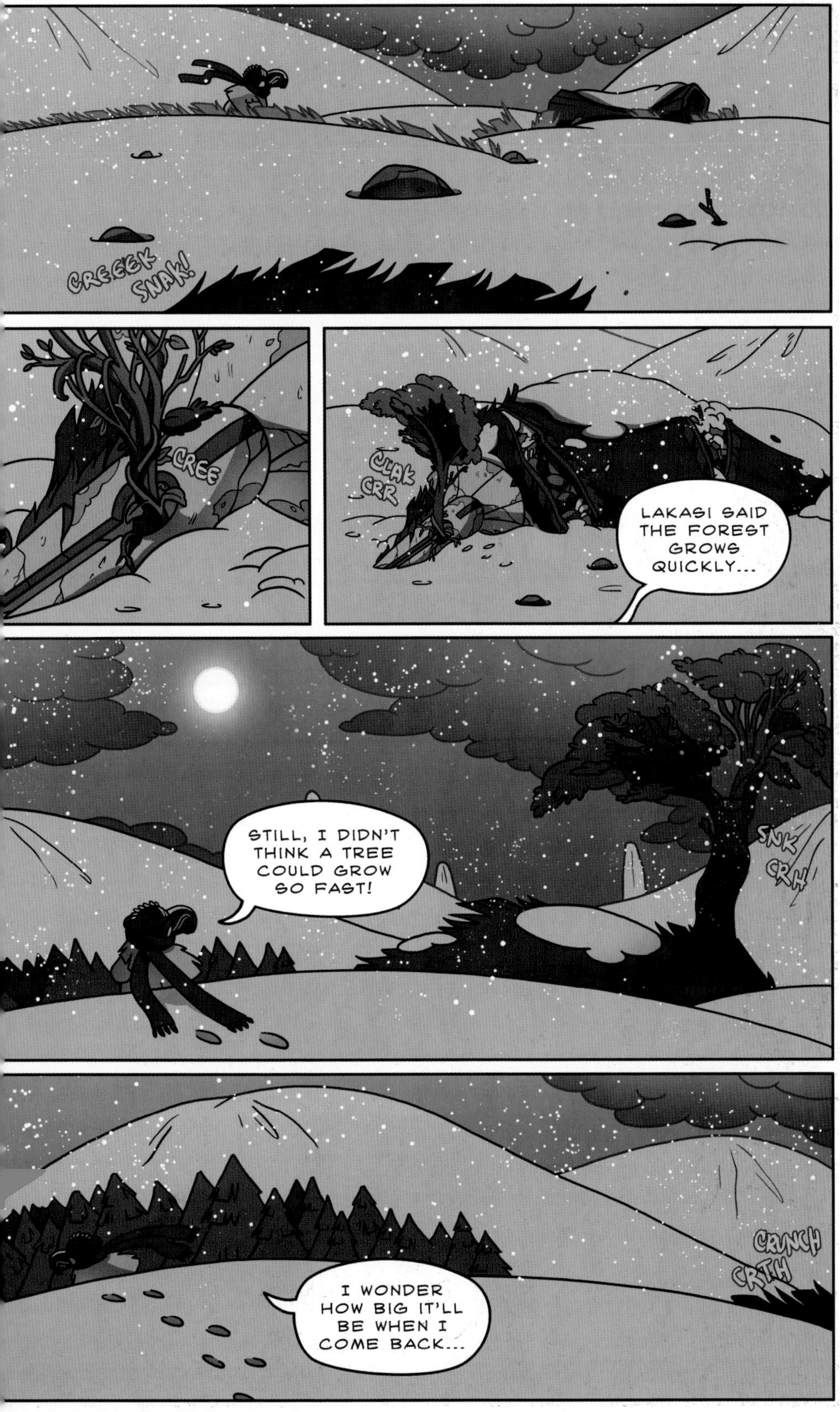
CREEEK
SNAK!
CREE
CLAK
CRR
LAKASI SAID THE FOREST GROWS QUICKLY...
STILL, I DIDN'T THINK A TREE COULD GROW SO FAST!
SNK
CRH
CRUNCH
CRTH
I WONDER HOW BIG IT'LL BE WHEN I COME BACK...

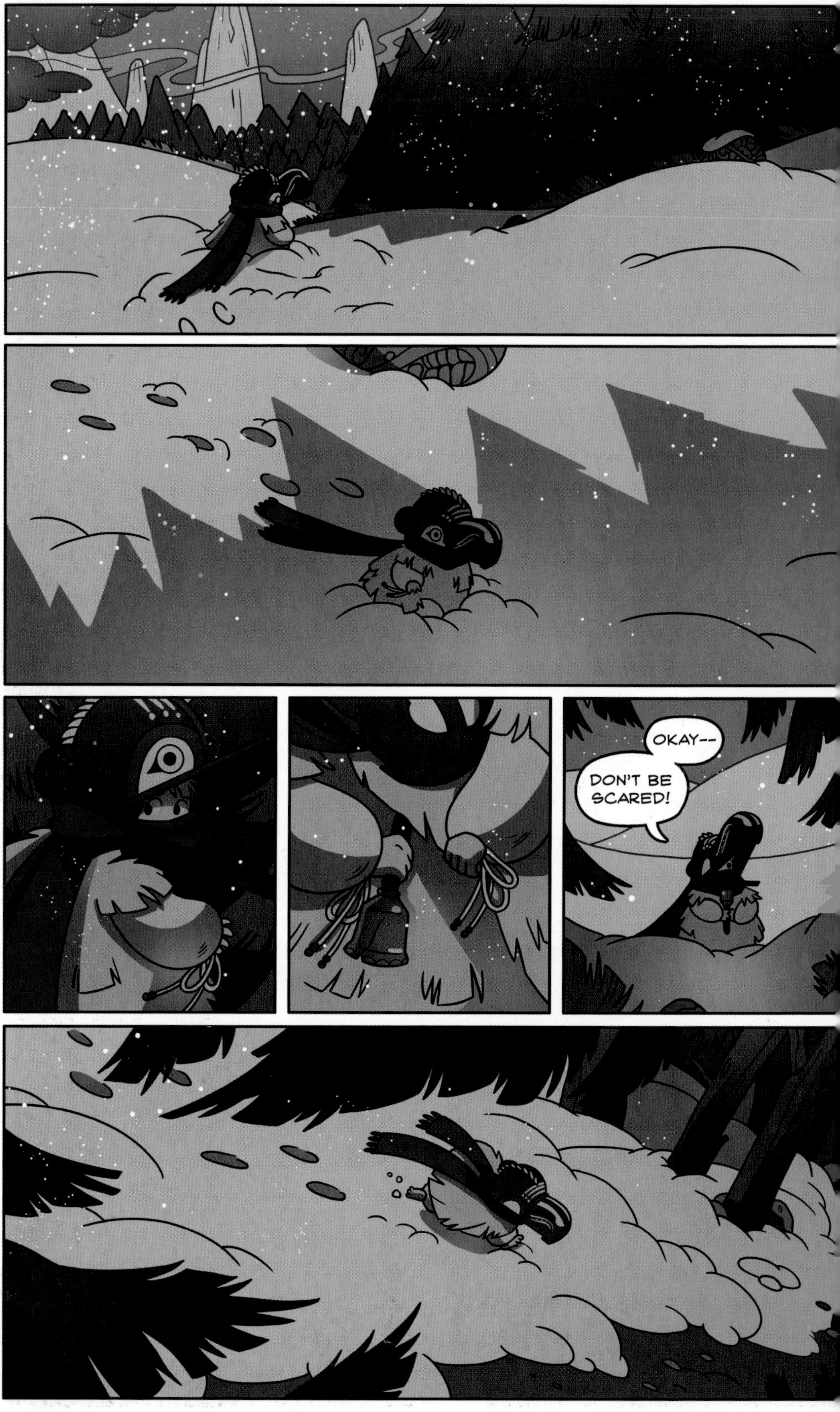
OKAY--
DON'T BE SCARED!

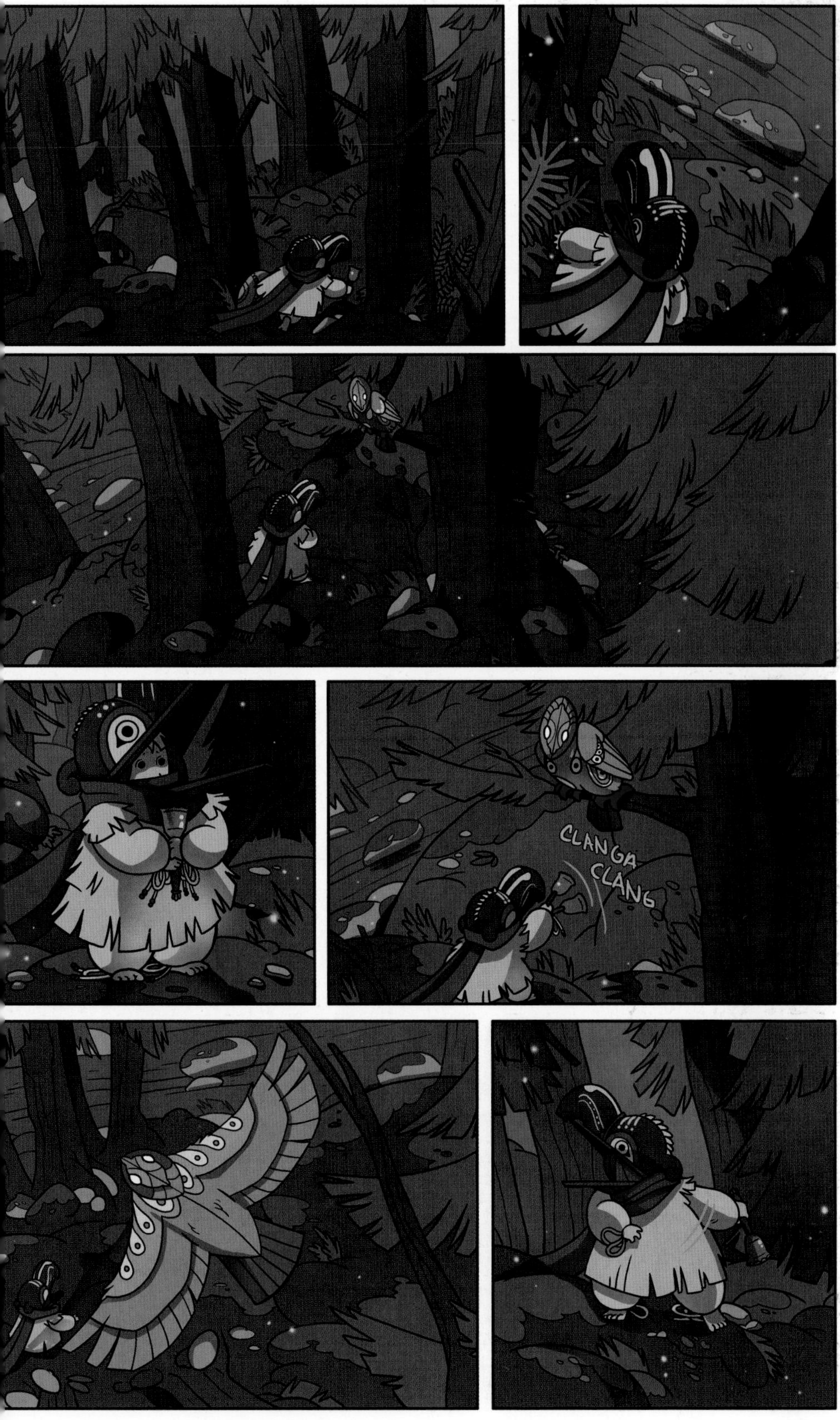
CLANGA
CLANG

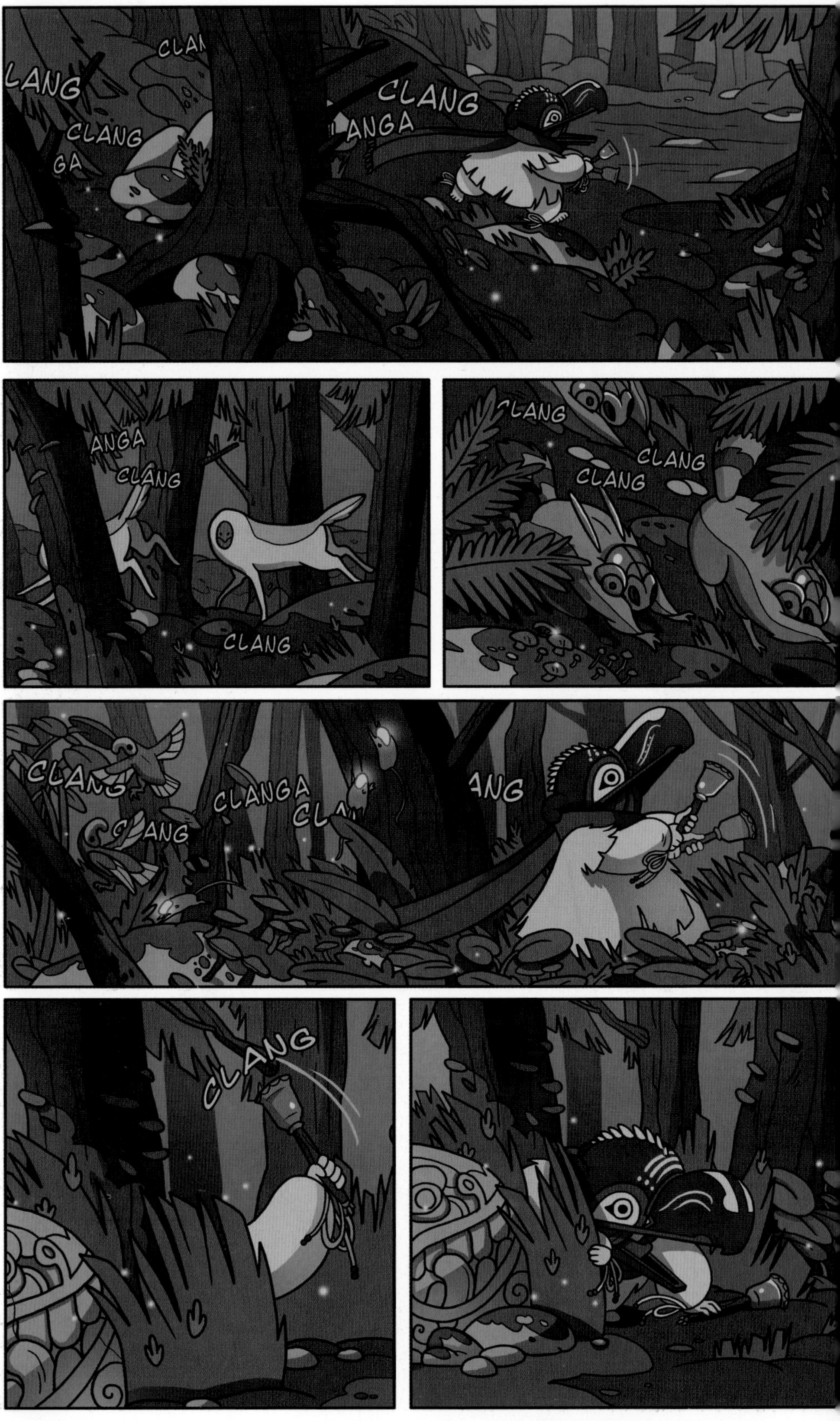
CLAN
LANG
CLANG
GA
CLANG
ANGA
ANGA
CLANG
CLANG
CLANG
CLANG
CLANG
CLANG
CLANGA
CLA
ANG
CLANG

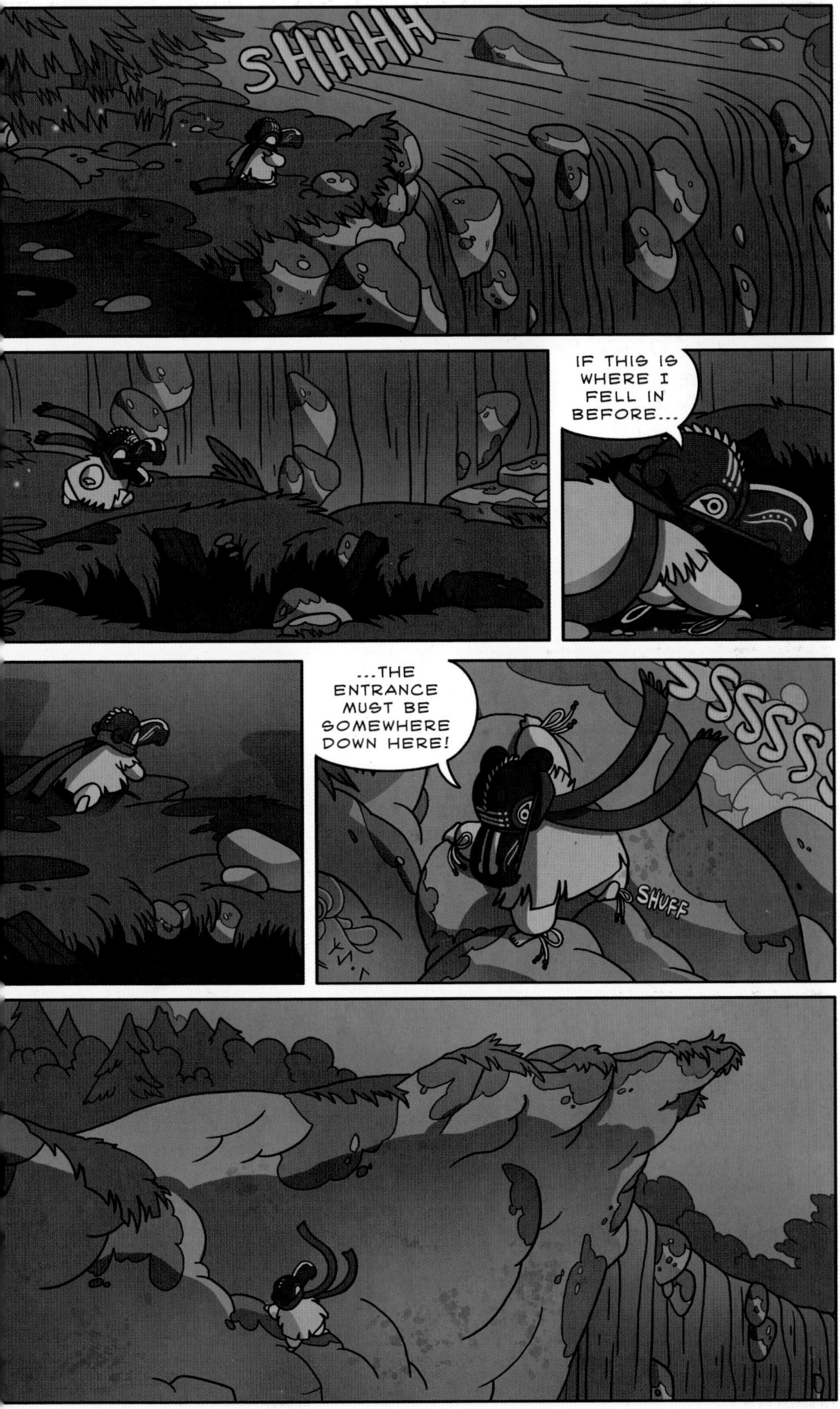
SHHHH
IF THIS IS WHERE I FELL IN BEFORE...
...THE ENTRANCE MUST BE SOMEWHERE DOWN HERE!
SSSSS
SHUFF

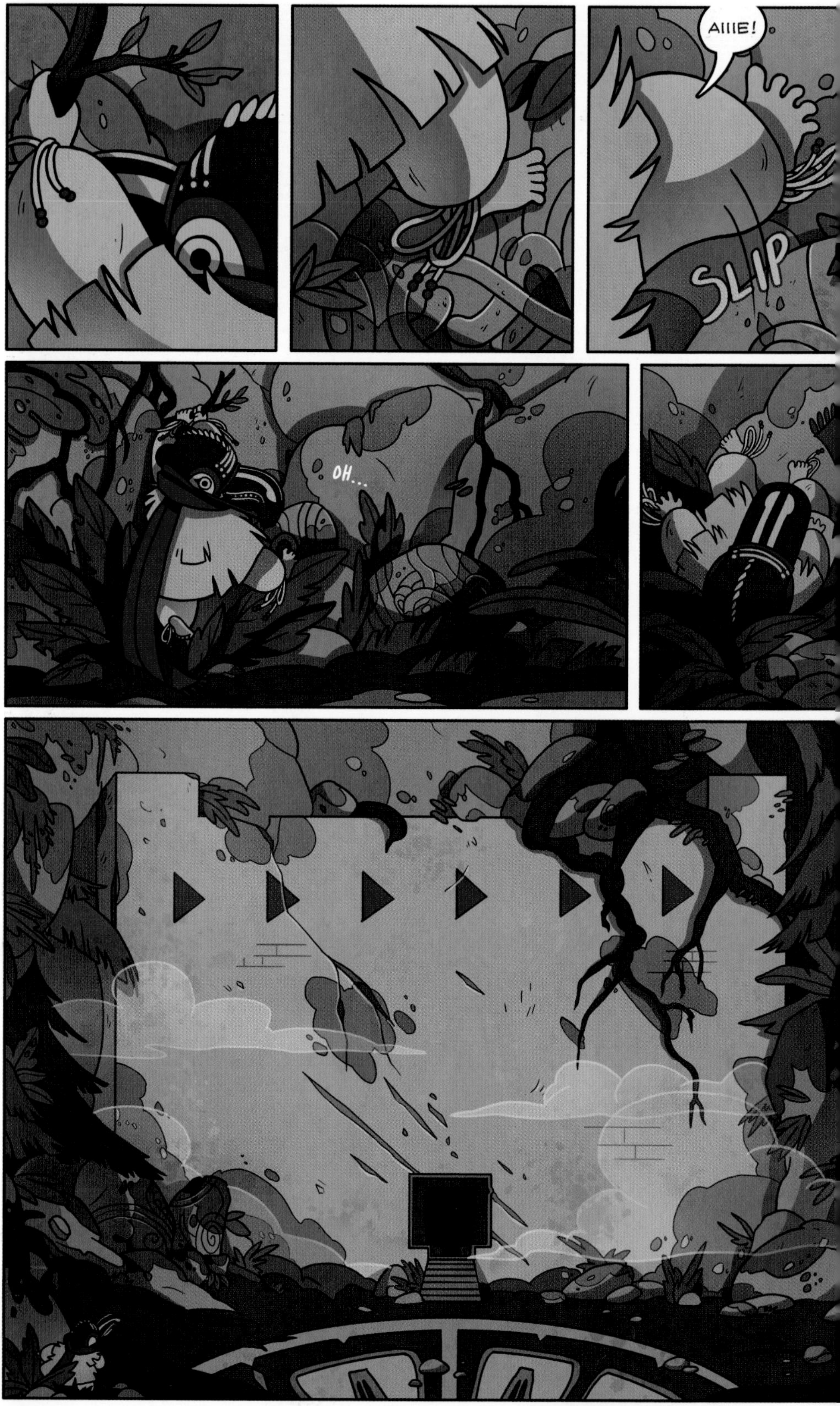
AIIIE!
SLIP
OH...

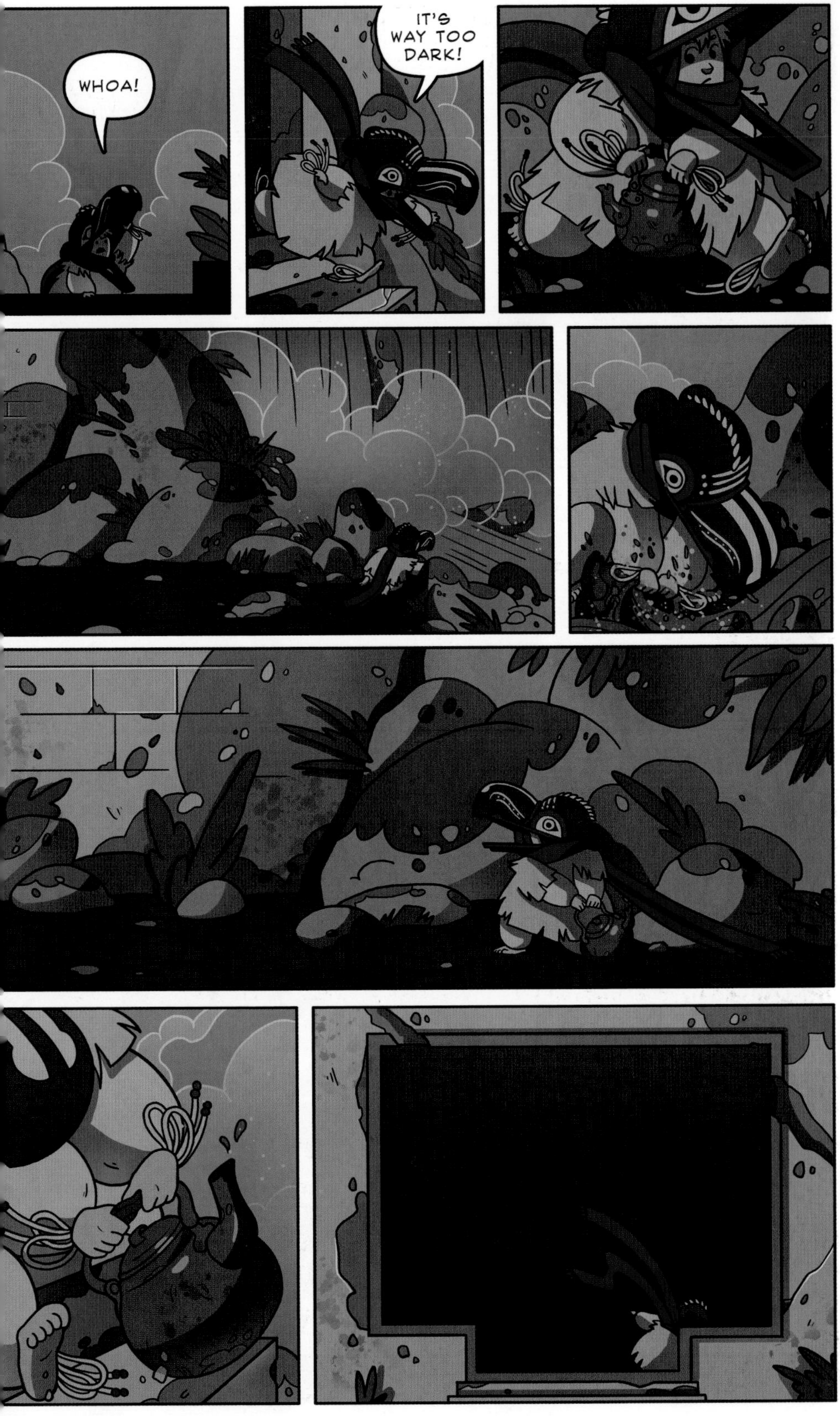
WHOA!
IT'S WAY TOO DARK!

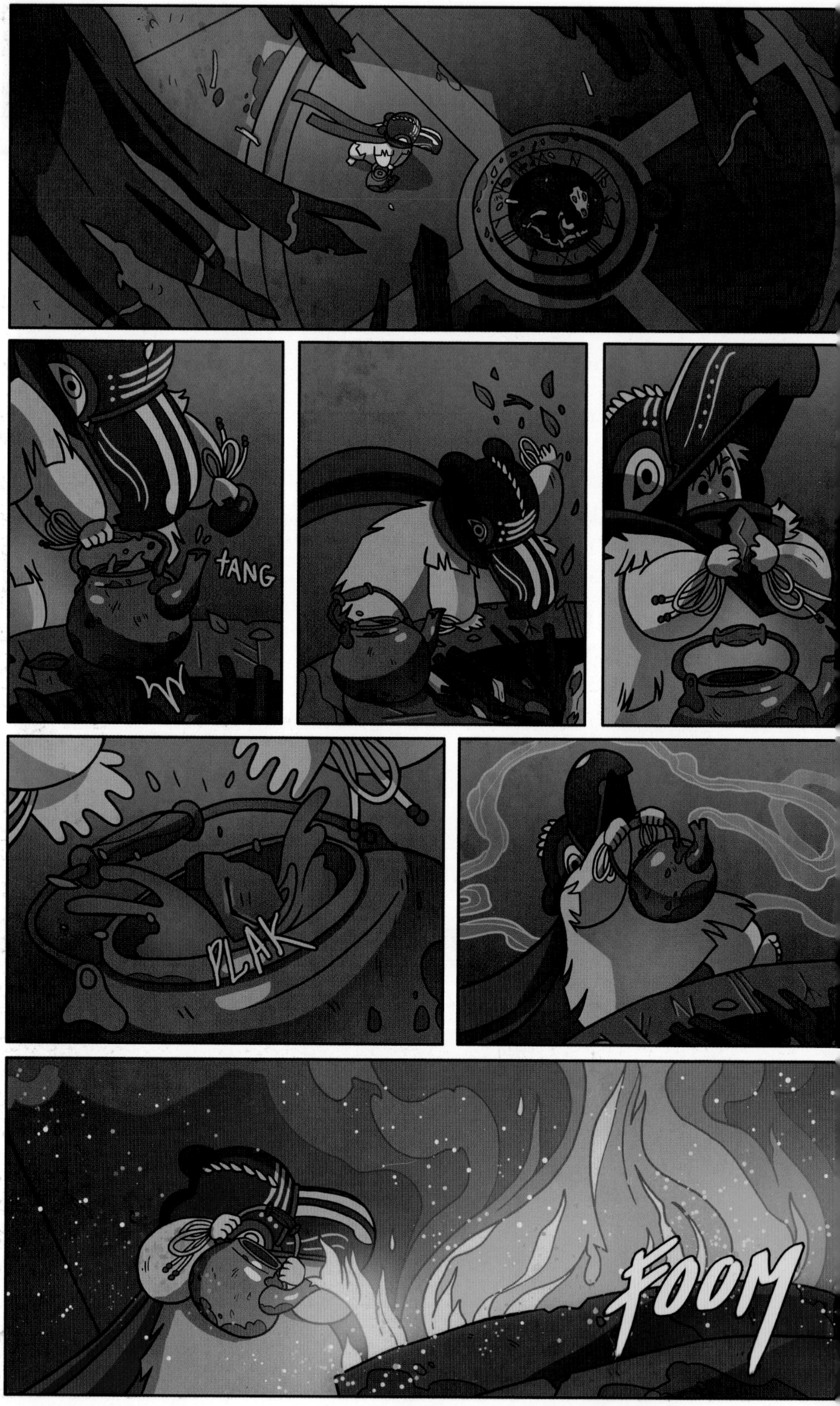
TANG
PLAK
FOOM

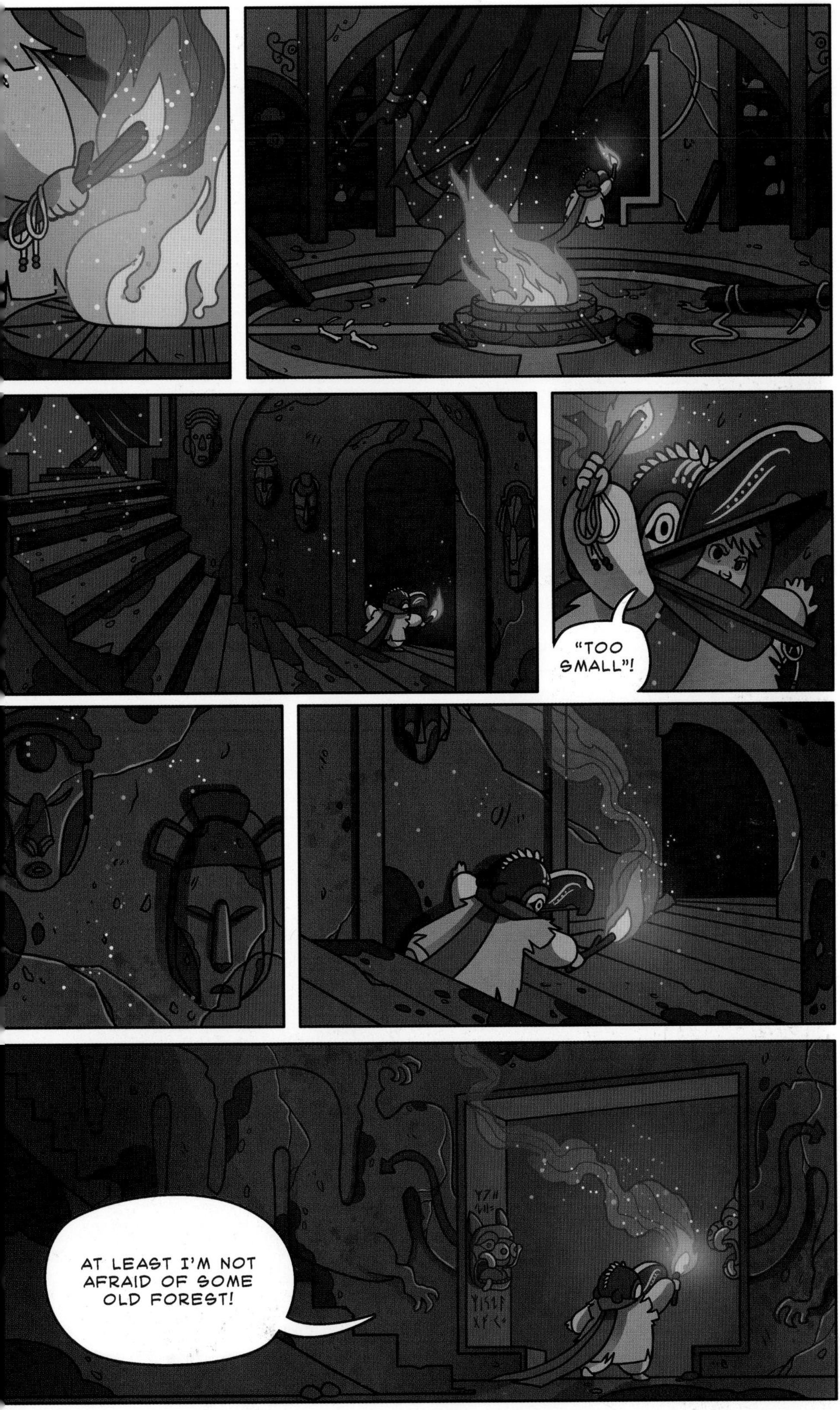
"TOO SMALL"!
AT LEAST I'M NOT AFRAID OF SOME OLD FOREST!

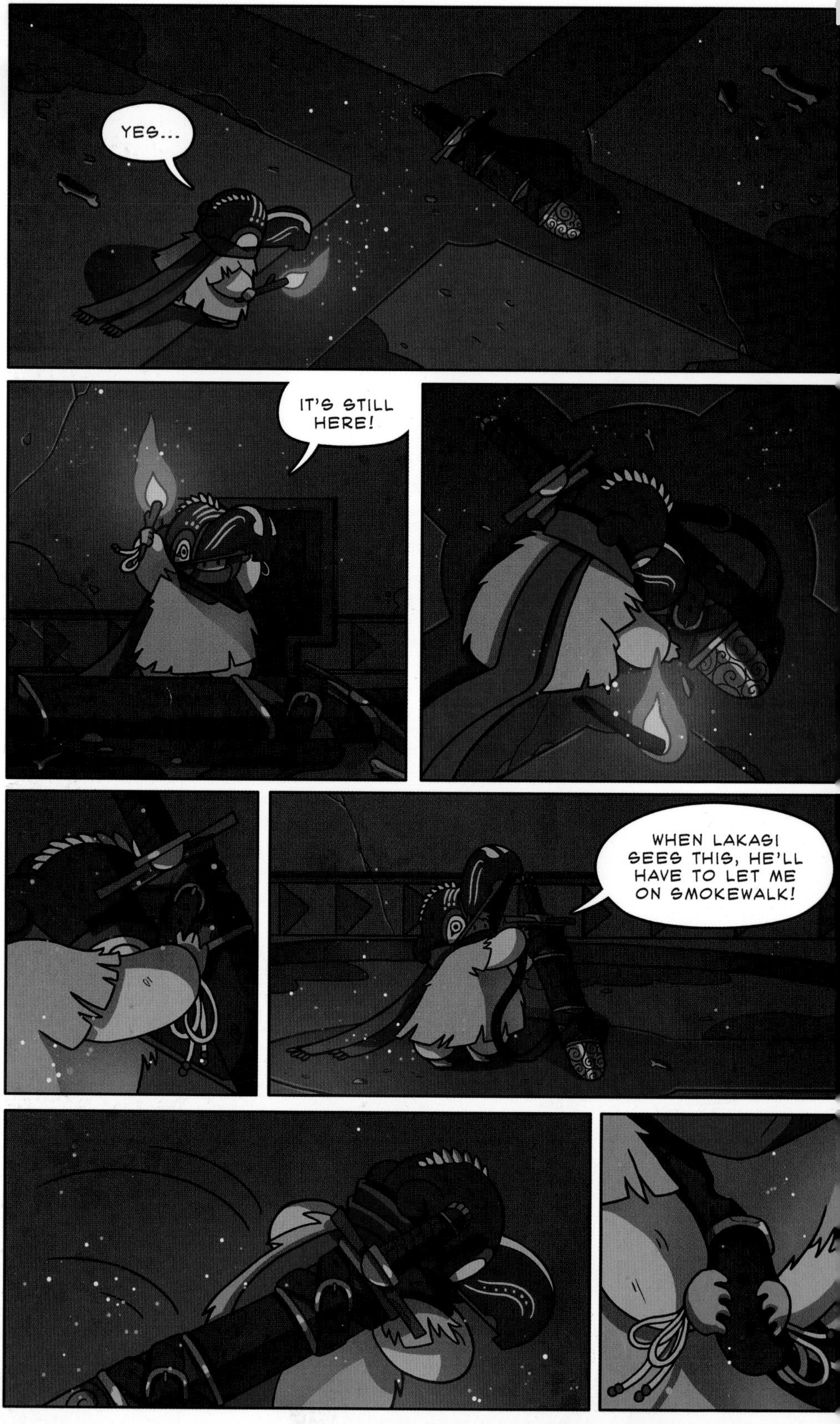
YES...
IT'S STILL HERE!
WHEN LAKASI SEES THIS, HE'LL HAVE TO LET ME ON SMOKEWALK!

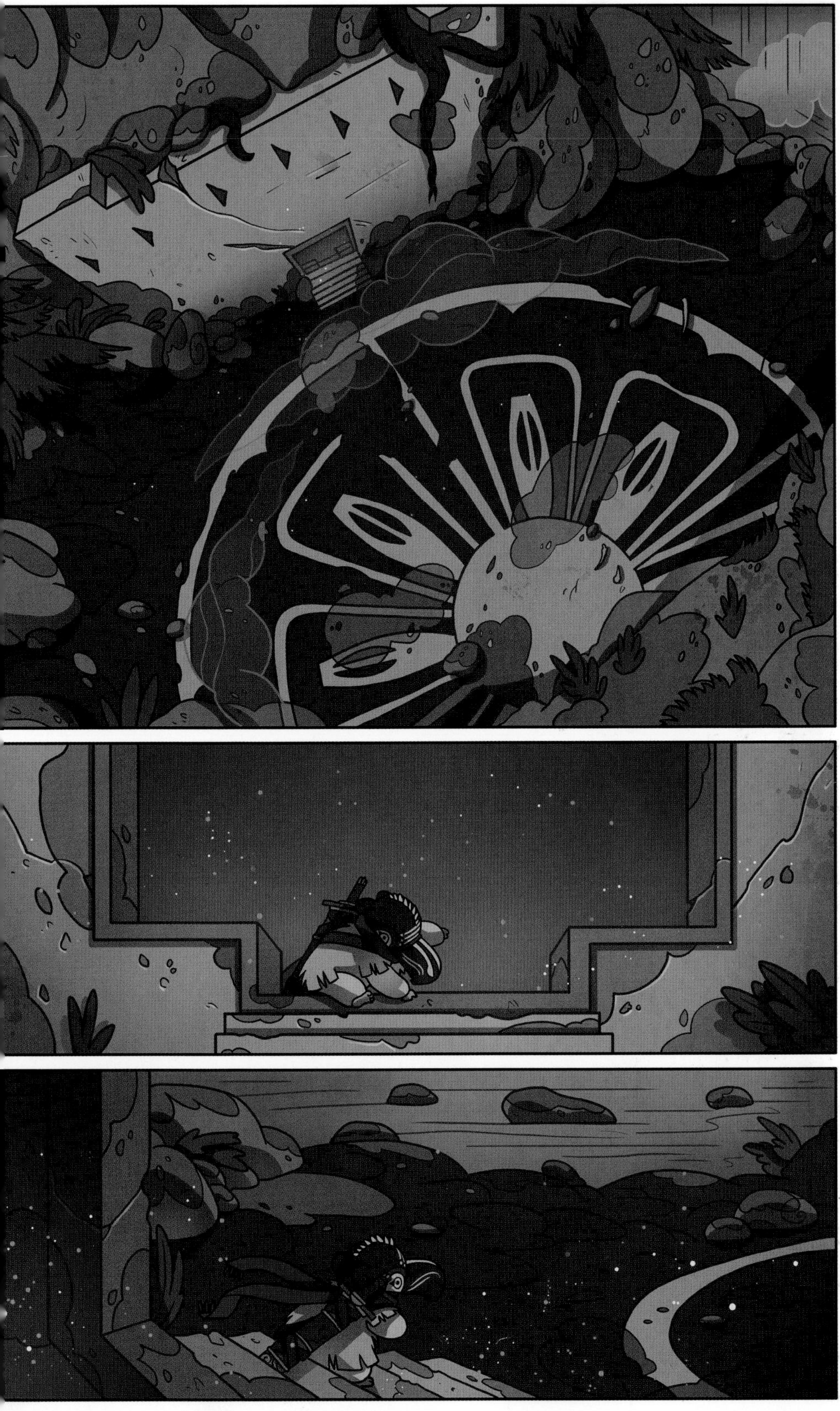

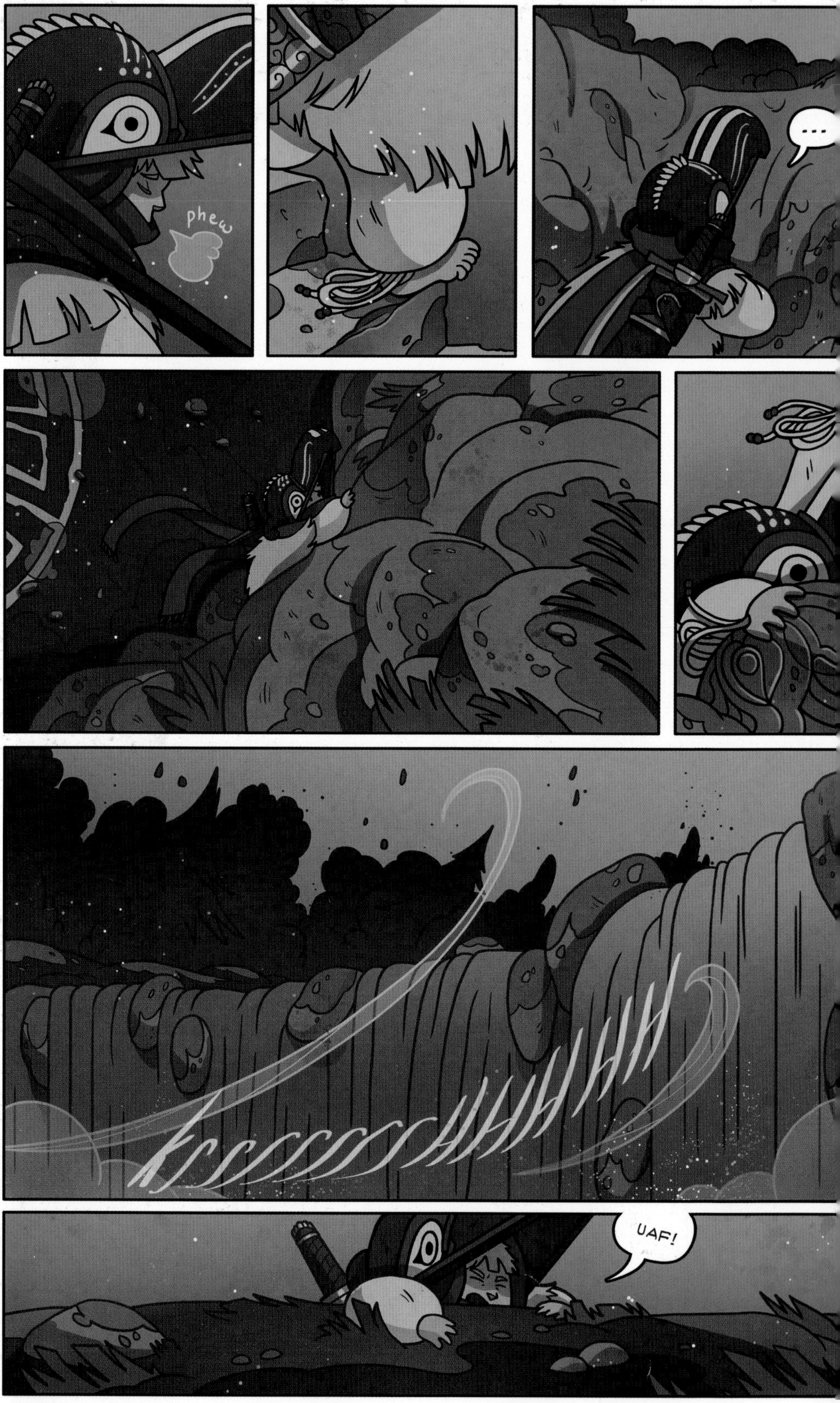
phew
...
UAF!

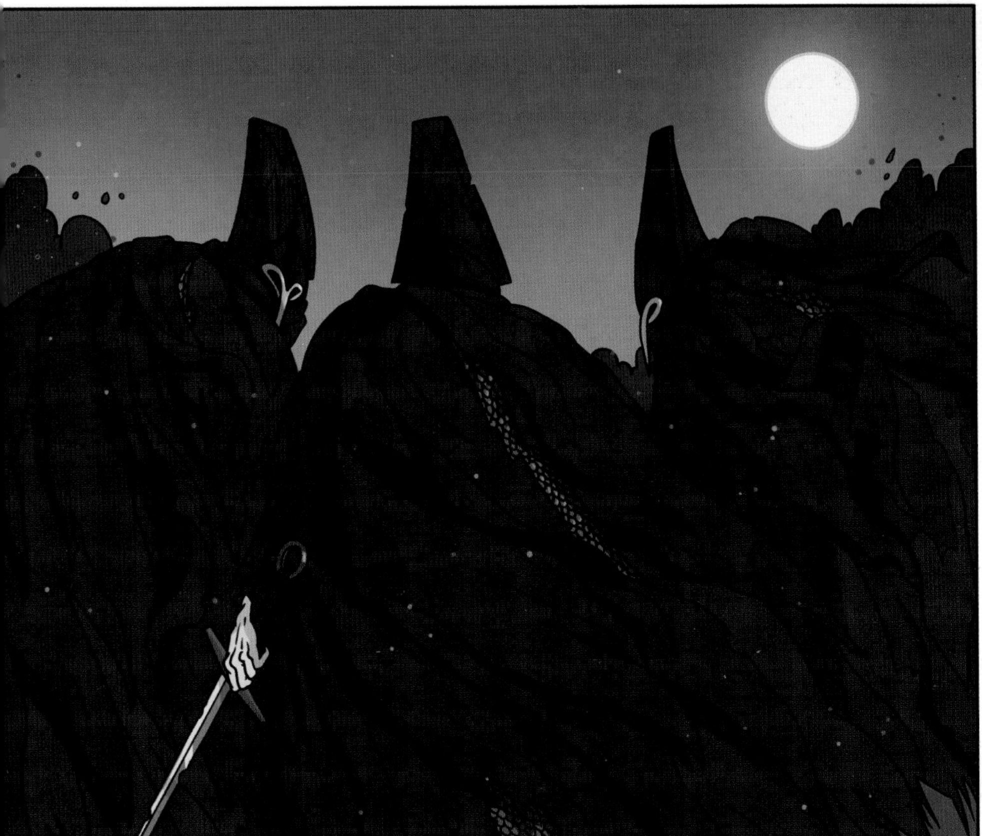
THE ROOK MEN CAME TO LIVE IN THE FOREST...

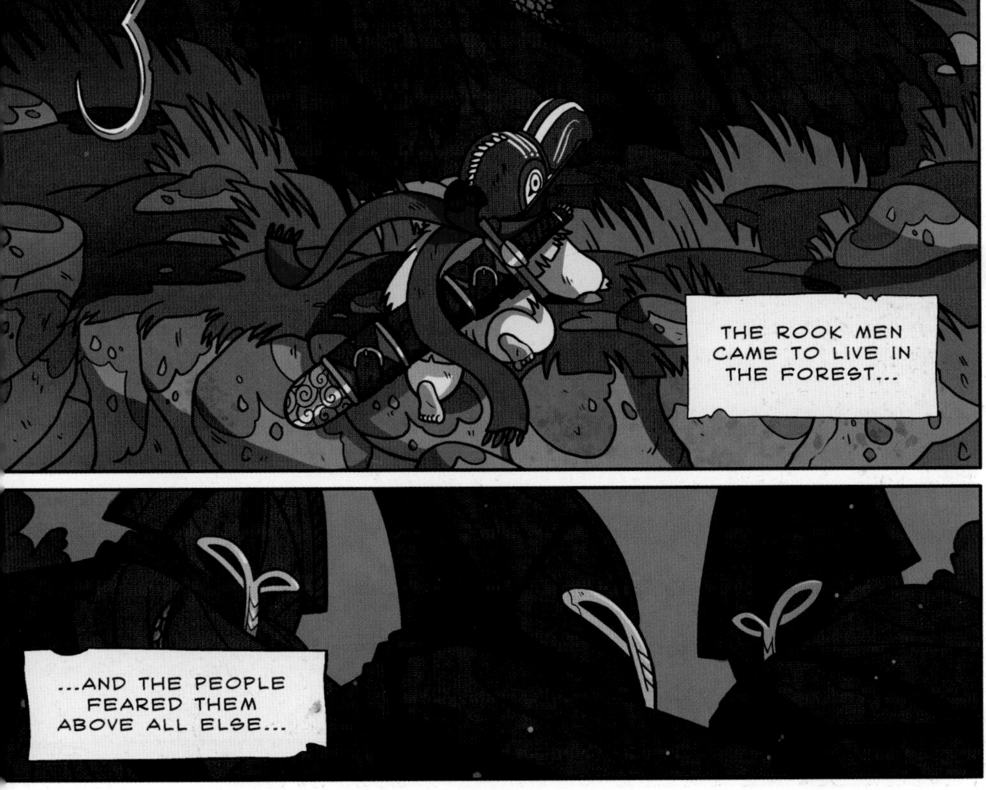
...AND THE PEOPLE FEARED THEM ABOVE ALL ELSE...

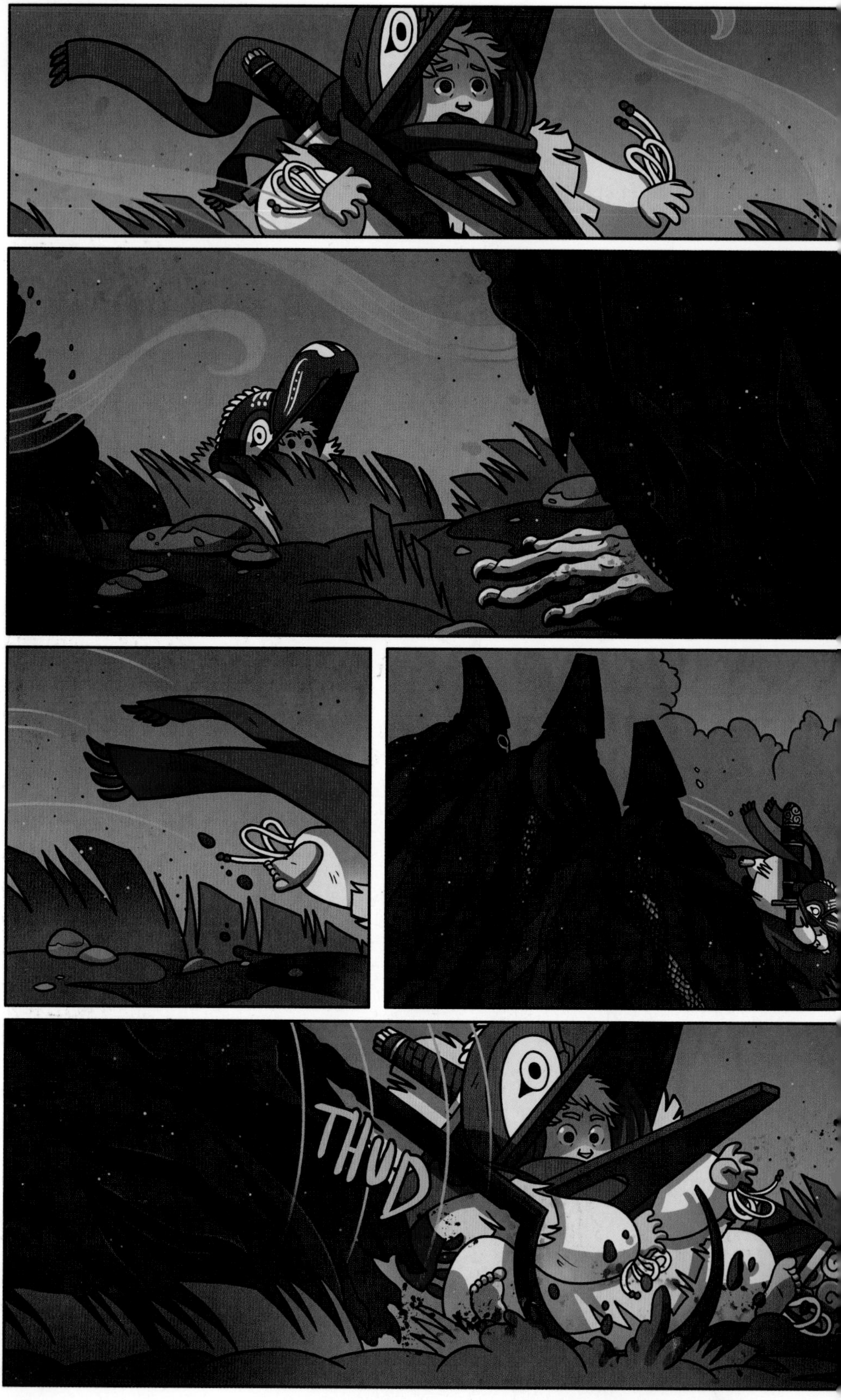
THUD

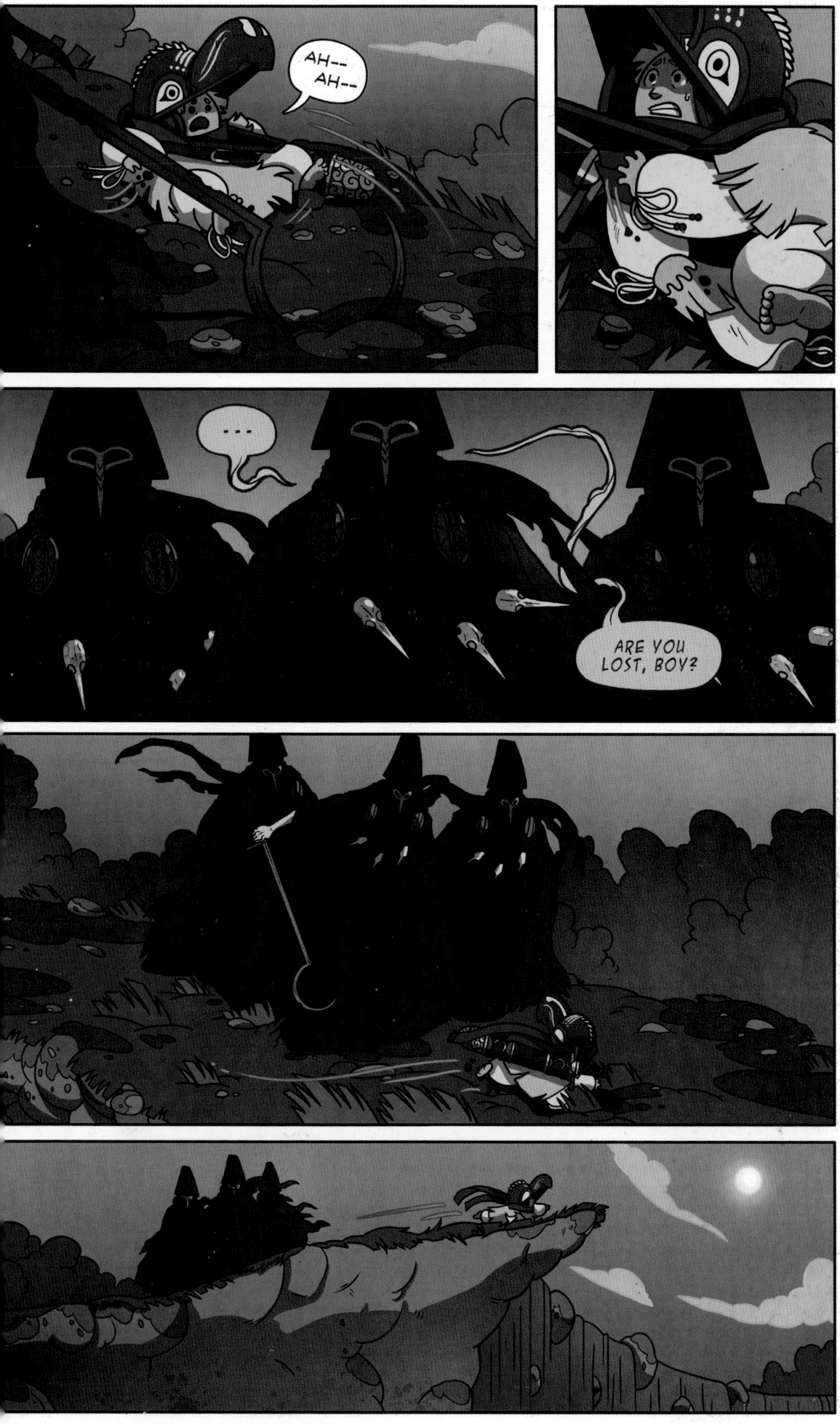
AH--
AH--
...
ARE YOU LOST, BOY?

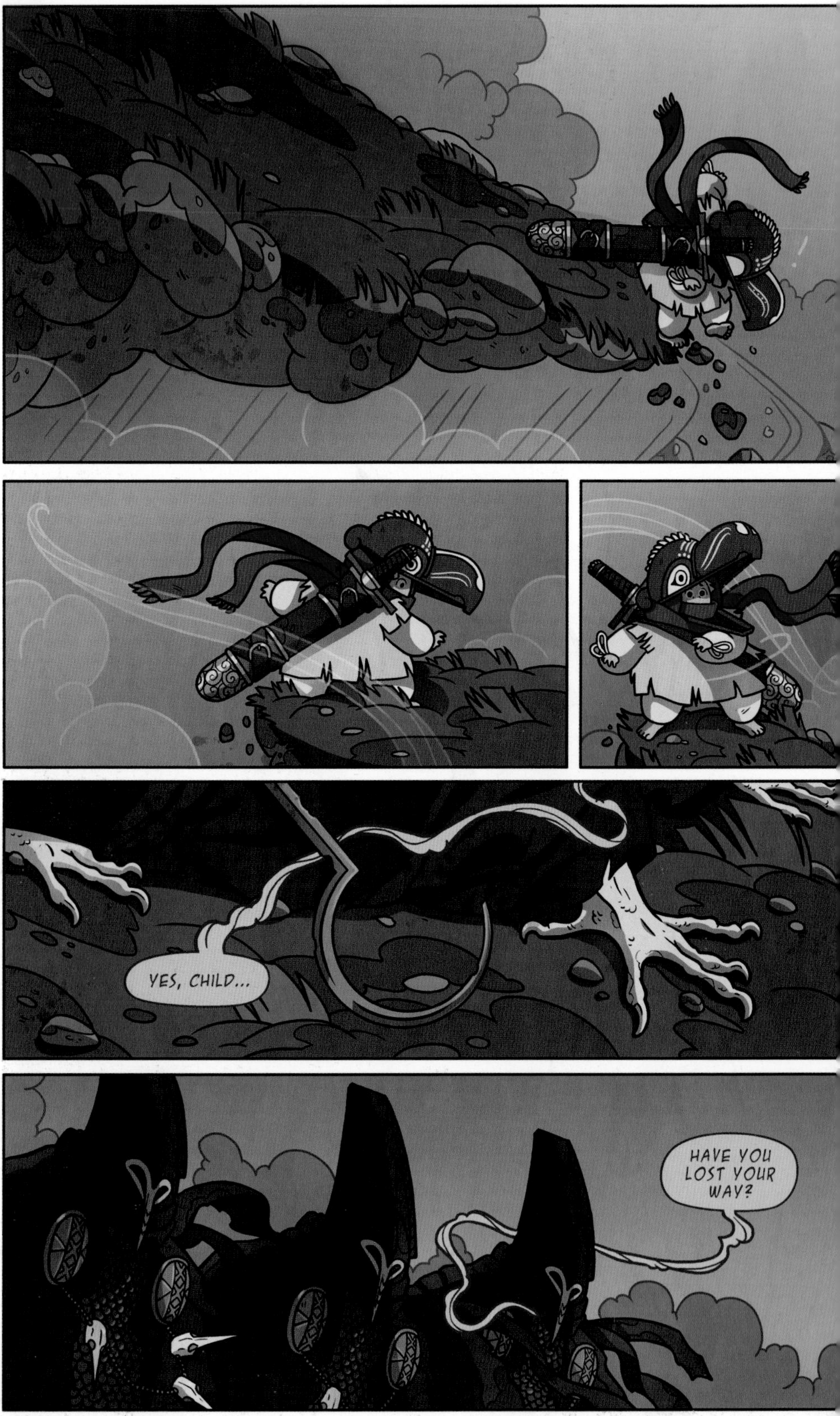
YES, CHILD...
HAVE YOU LOST YOUR WAY?

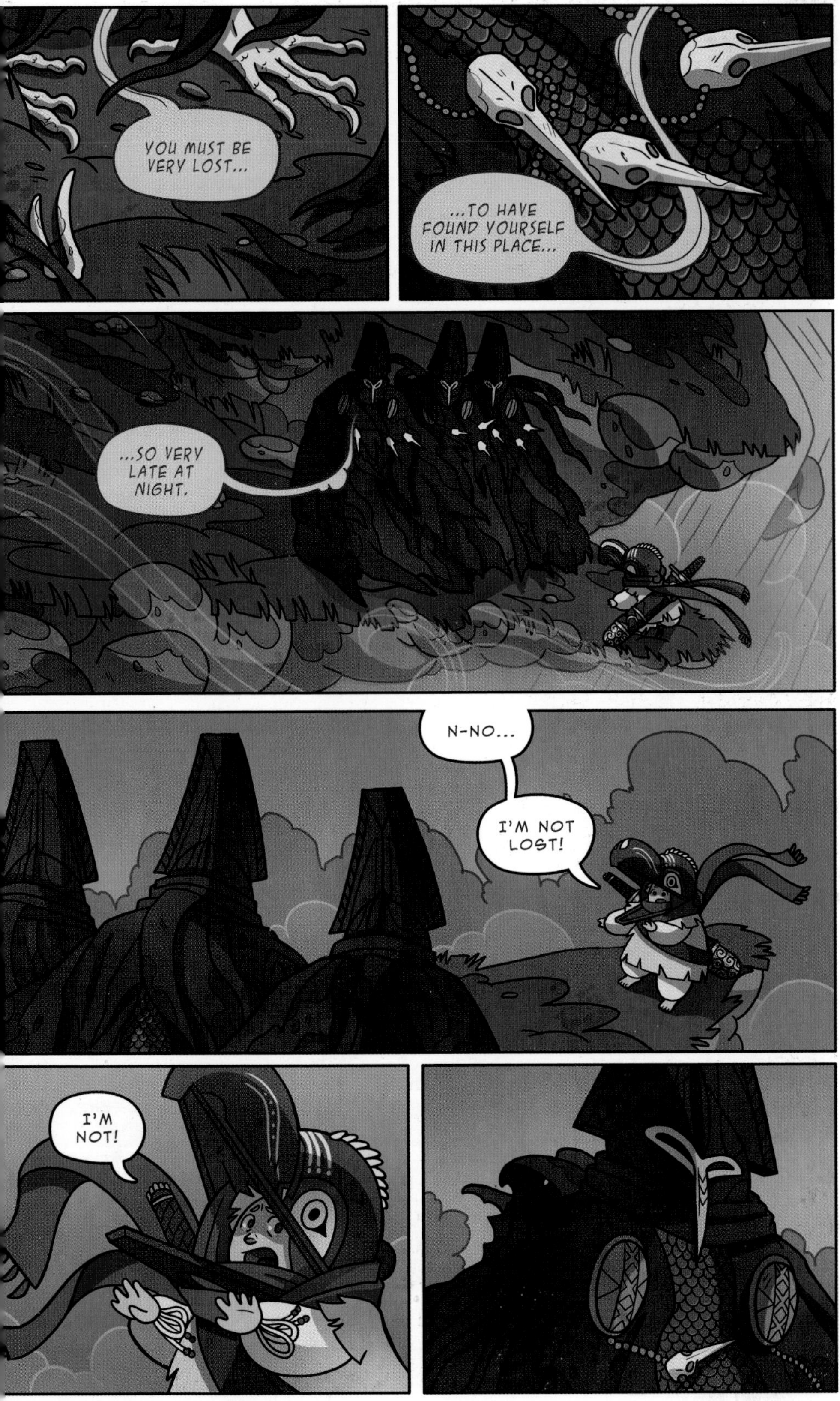
YOU MUST BE VERY LOST...
...TO HAVE FOUND YOURSELF IN THIS PLACE...
...SO VERY LATE AT NIGHT.
N-NO...
I'M NOT LOST!
I'M NOT!

WE ARE THE KEEPERS OF THOSE WHO ARE LOST...
THOSE WHO DARE ENTER THIS FOREST MUST ALL BE LOST...
AND SO WE KEEP THEM ALL.
NOW, BOY, COME WITH US.
YES.
YES.
NOW.

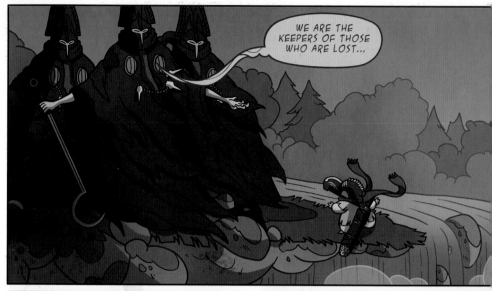

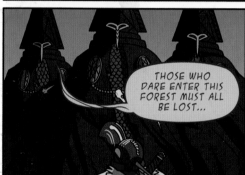

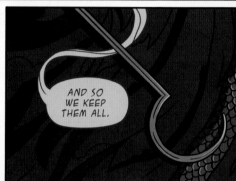

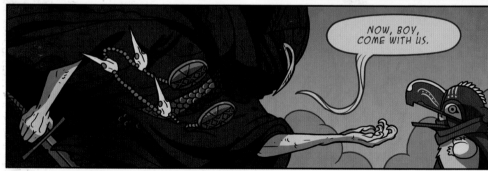

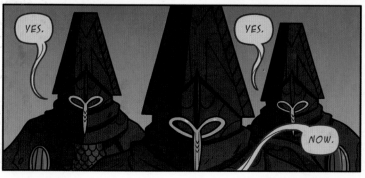

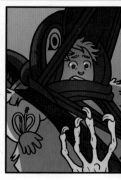

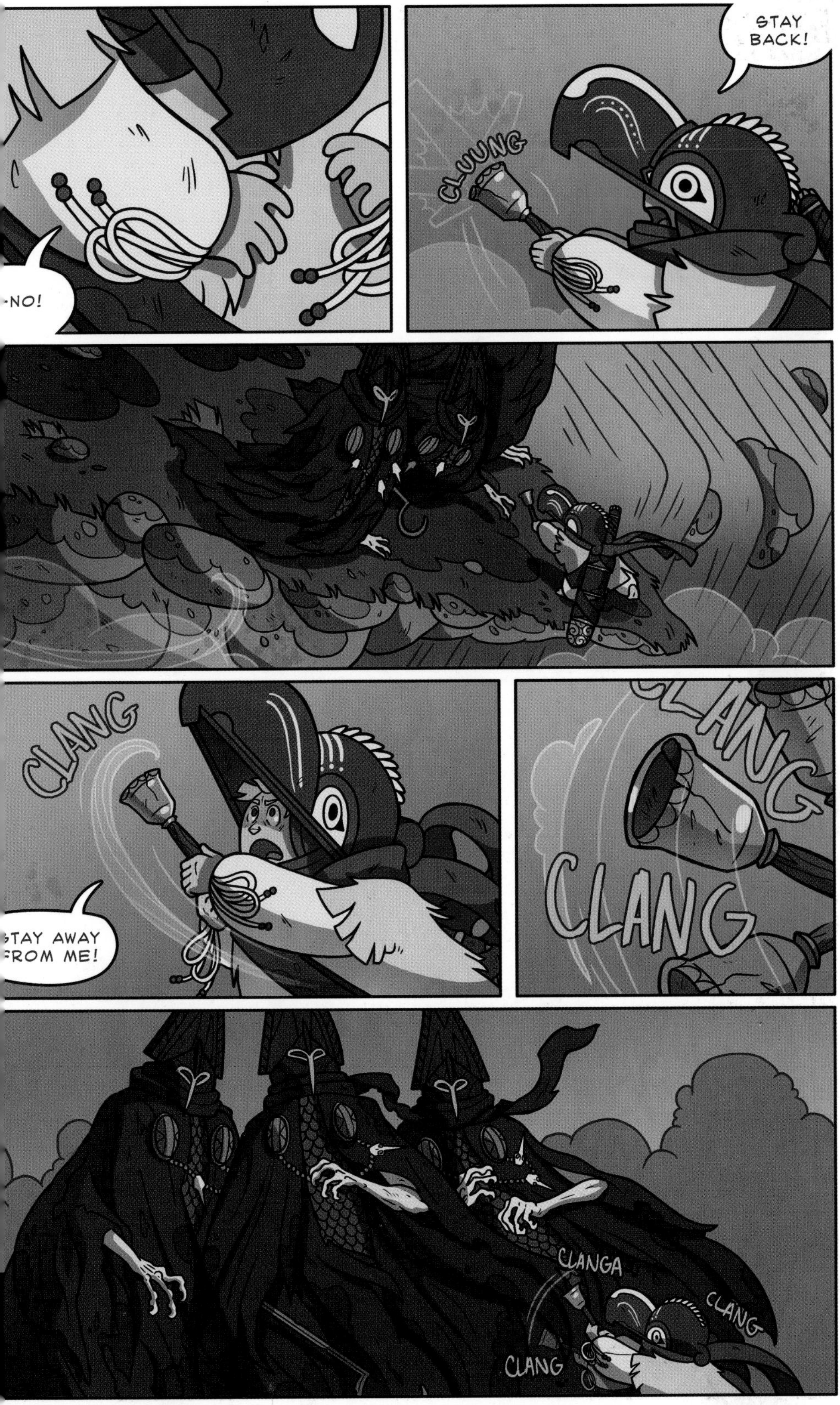
-NO!
STAY BACK!
CLUUNG
CLANG
STAY AWAY FROM ME!
CLANG
CLANG
CLANGA
CLANG
CLANG

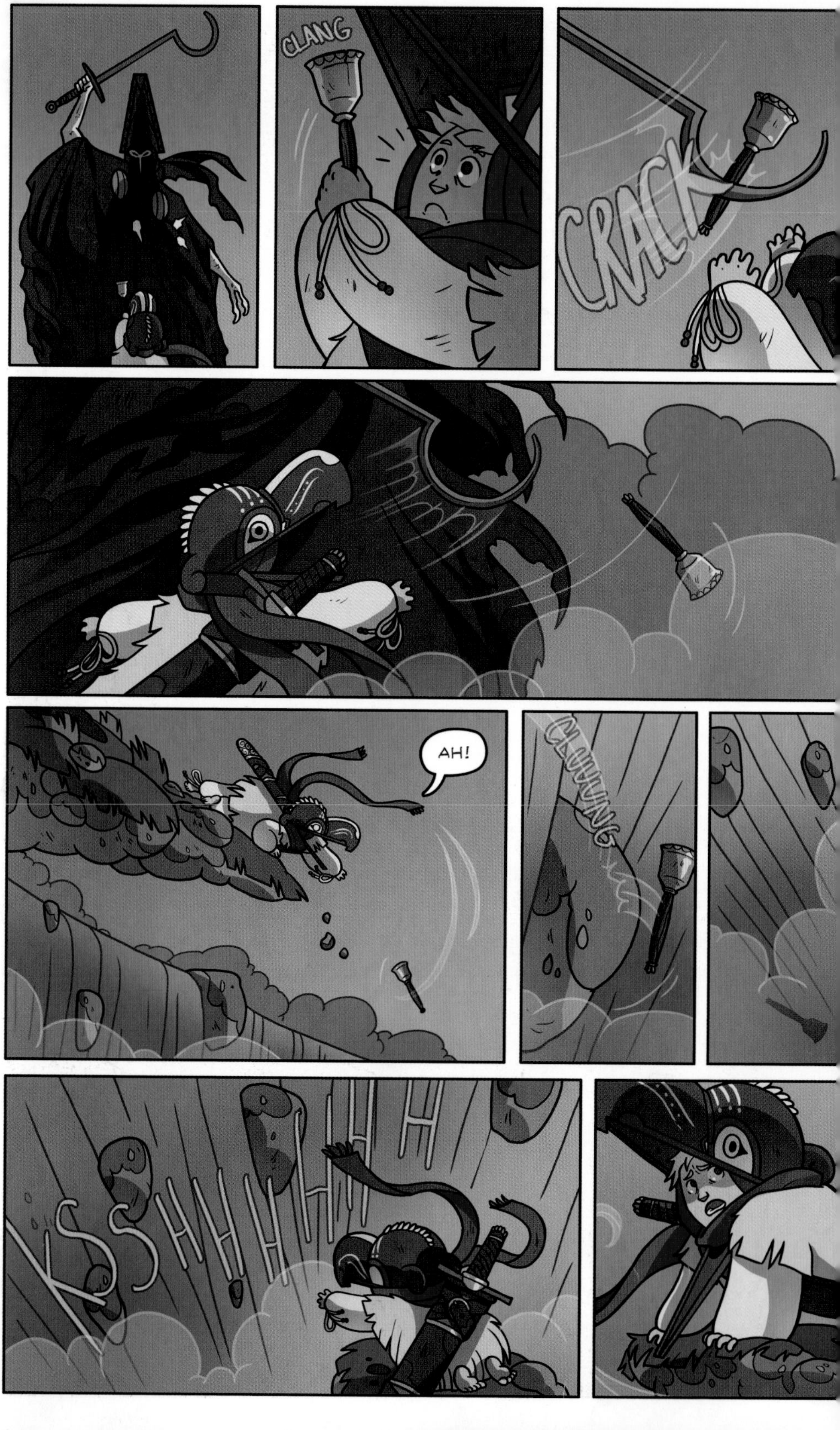
CLANG
CRACK
AH!
CLUUUNG
KSSHHHHHH

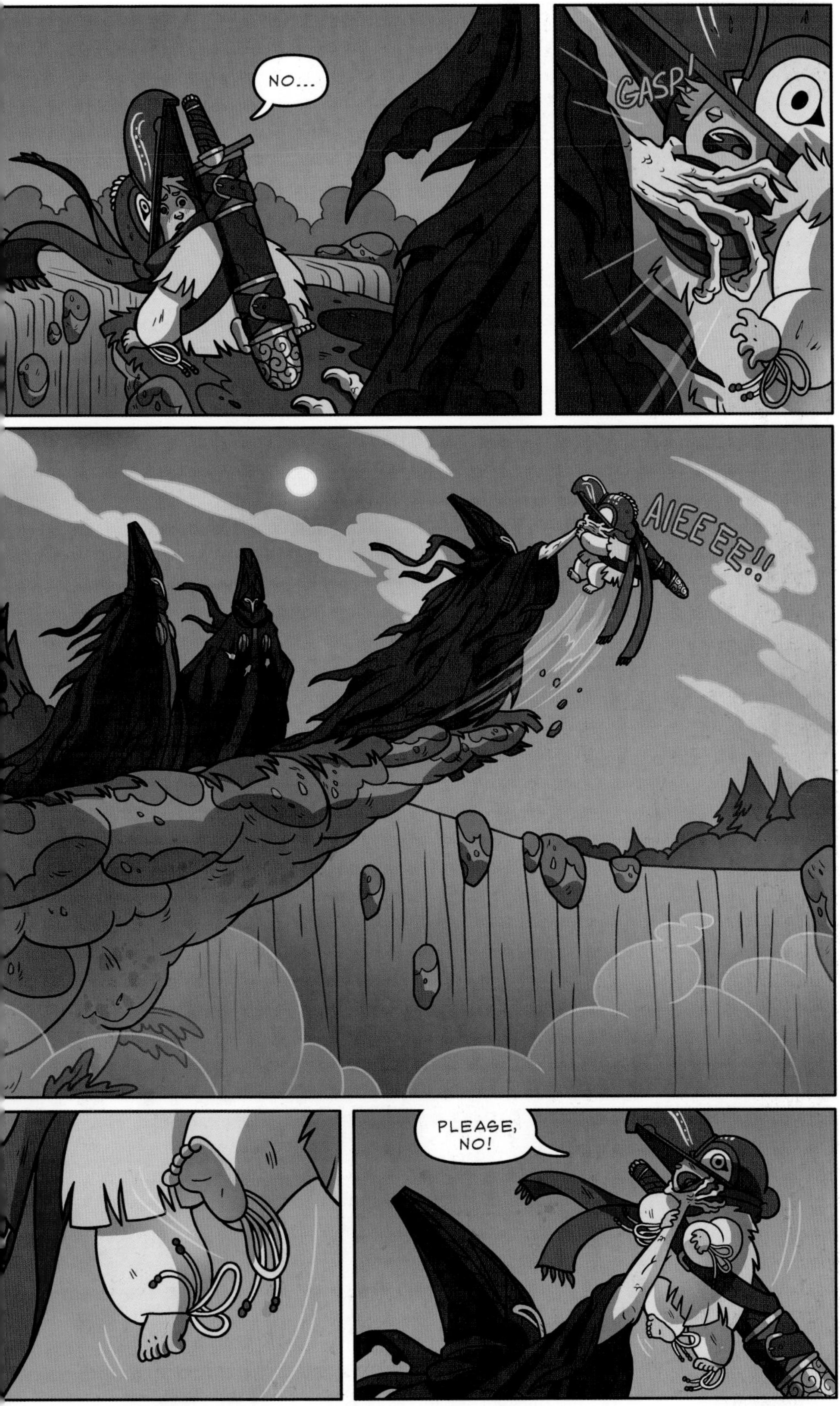
NO...
GASP!
AIEEEEE!!
PLEASE, NO!

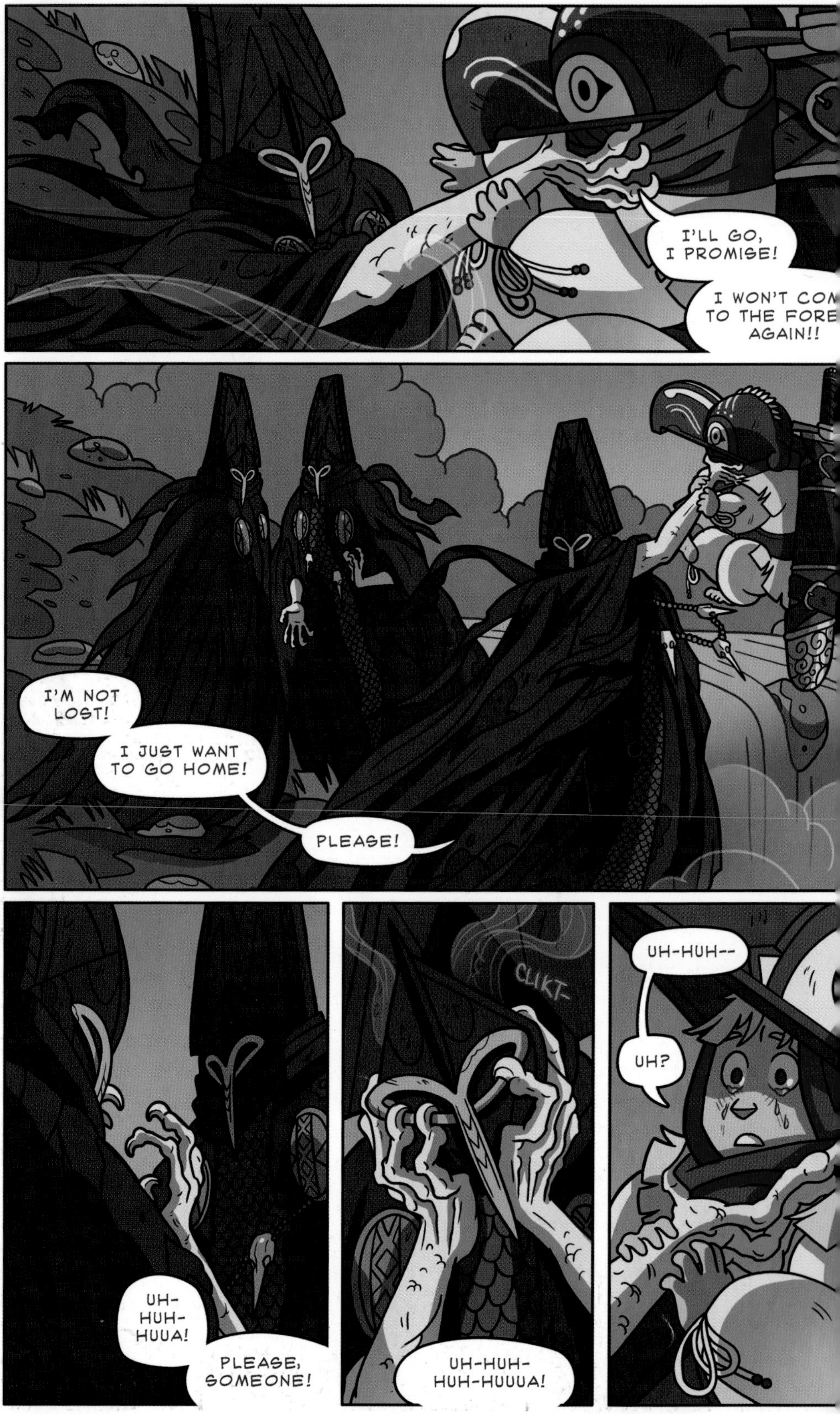
I'LL GO, I PROMISE!
I WON'T COM TO THE FORE AGAIN!!
I'M NOT LOST!
I JUST WANT TO GO HOME!
PLEASE!
UH-HUH-HUUA!
PLEASE, SOMEONE!
CLIKT-
UH-HUH-HUH-HUUUA!
UH-HUH--
UH?

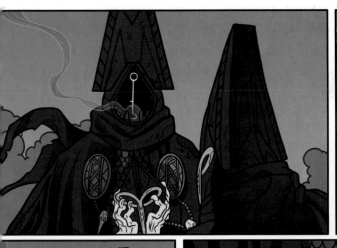

DO NOT DESPAIR, CHILD.

YOUR SACRIFICE WILL NOT BE WASTED.

SA--

SACRIFICE?!

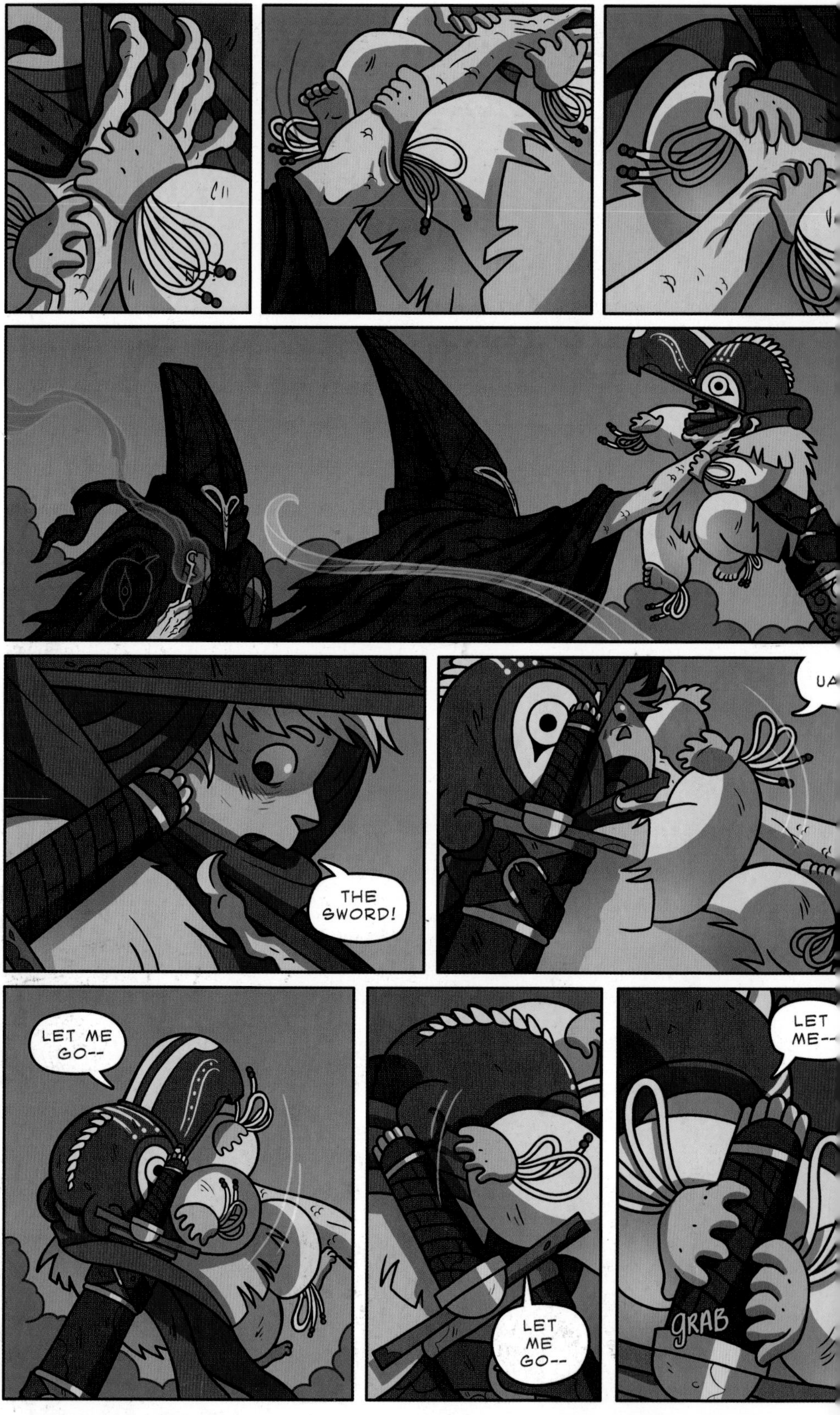
THE SWORD!
UA
LET ME GO--
LET ME GO--
LET ME--
GRAB

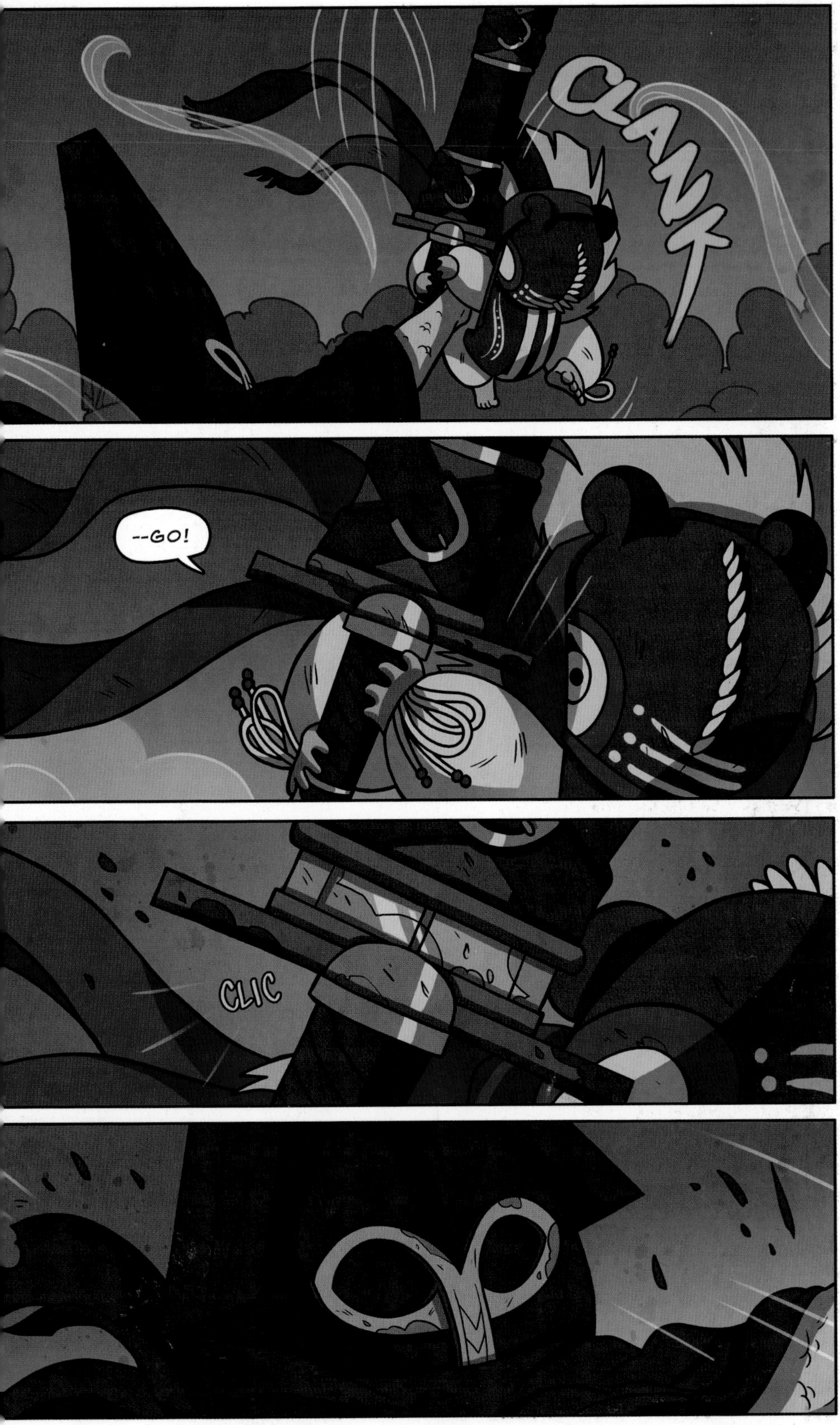
CLANK
--GO!
CLIC

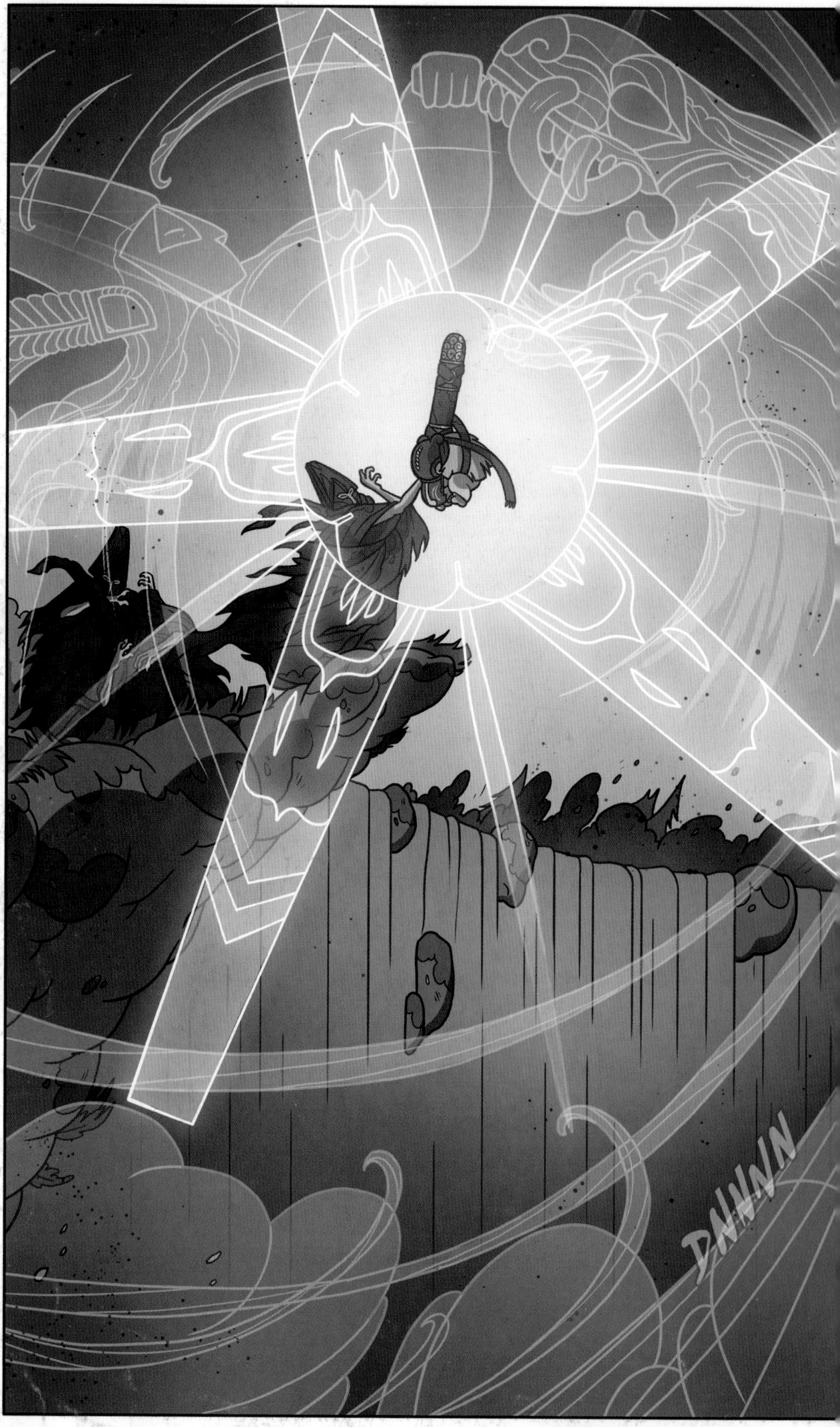
DNNNN

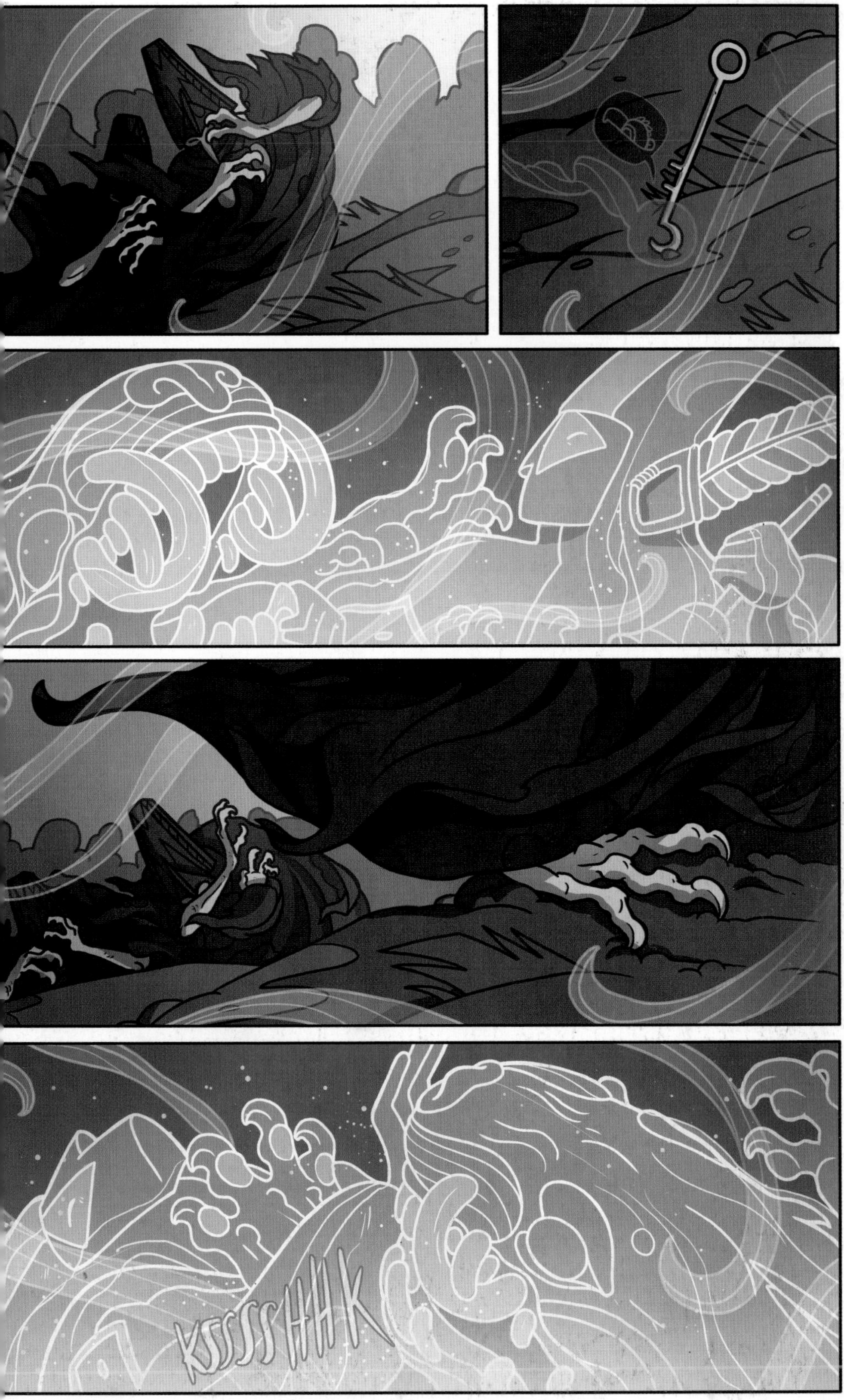
KSSSSSHHHK

RATTLE

RATTL.

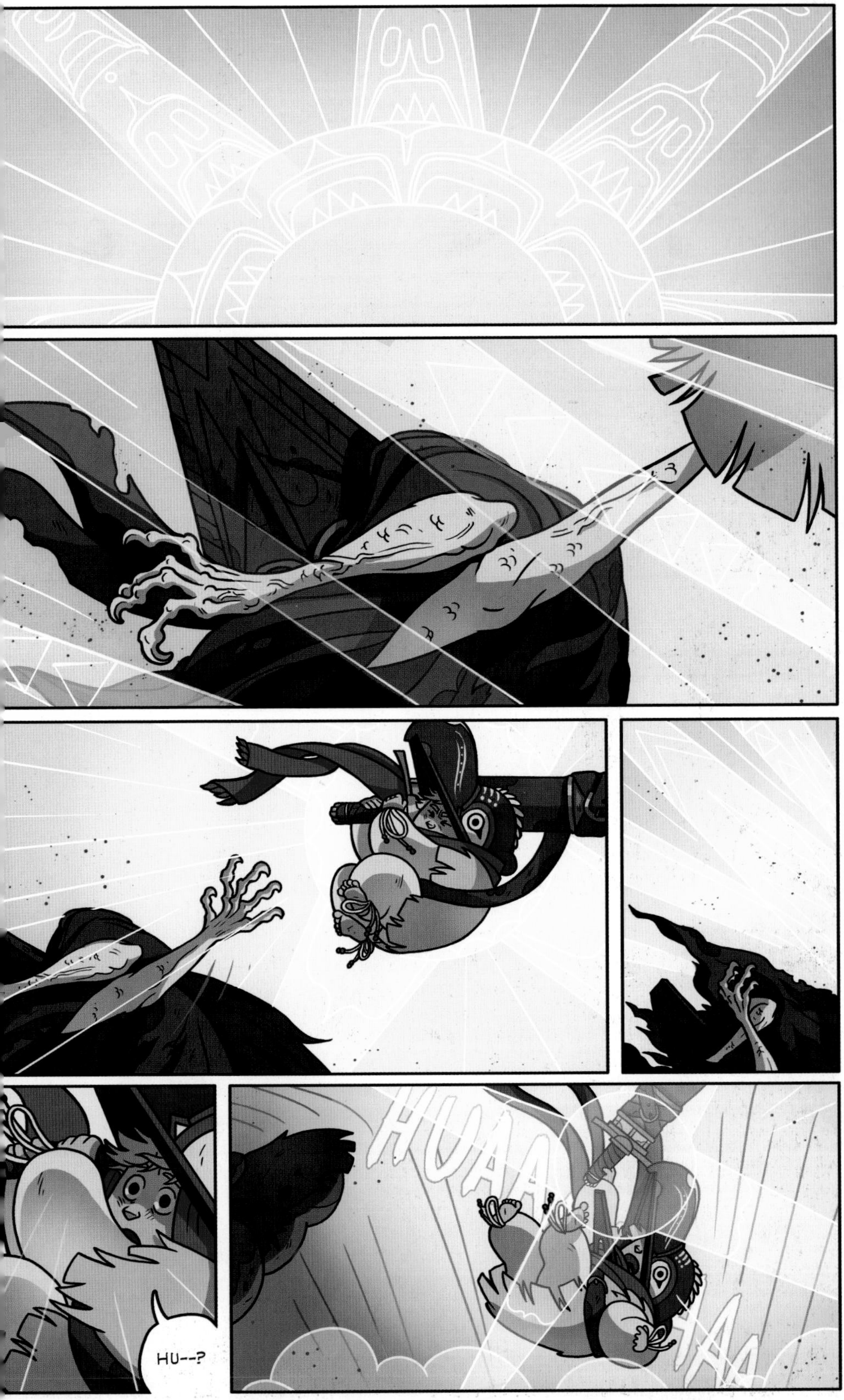
HUAA
AAA
HU--?

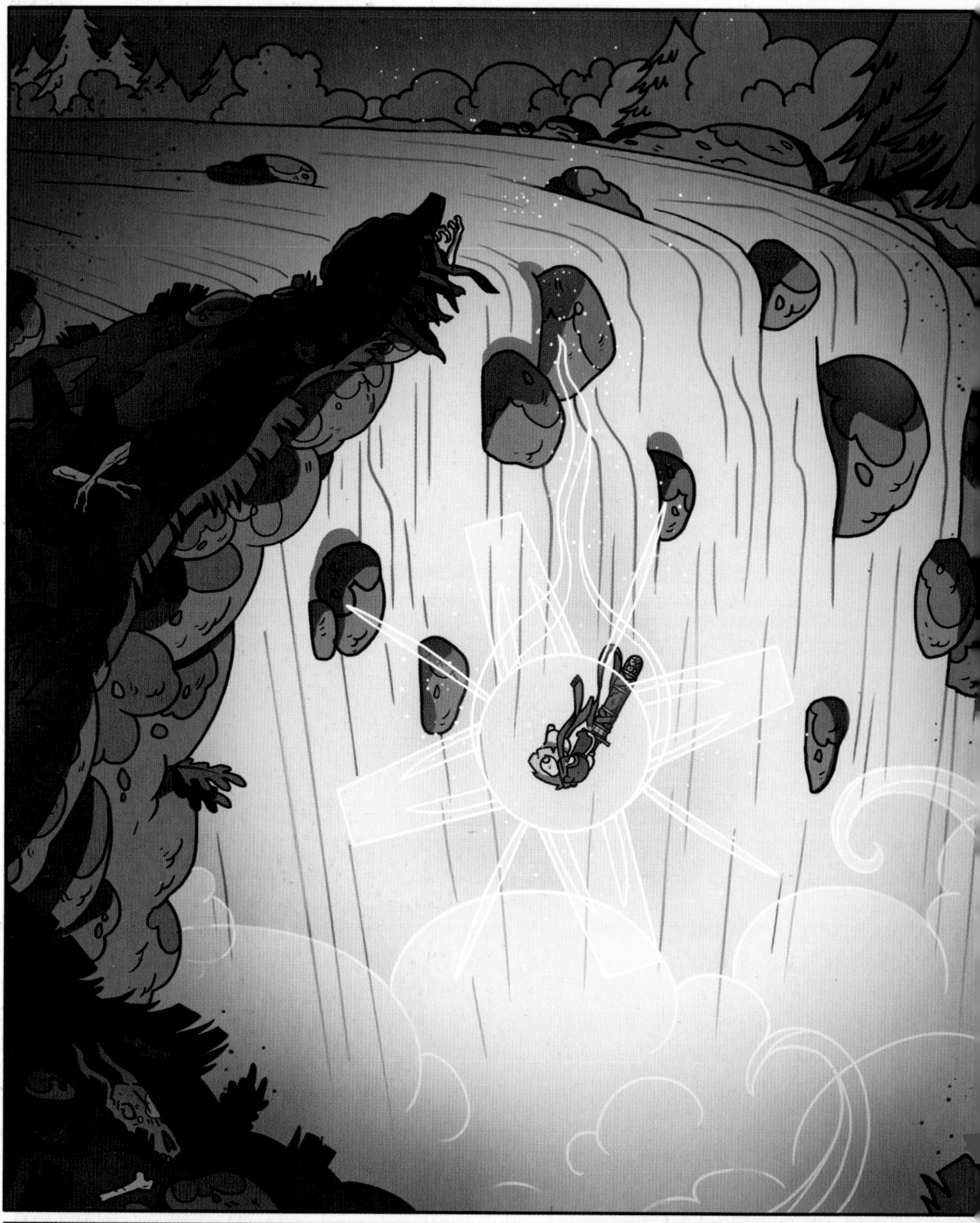

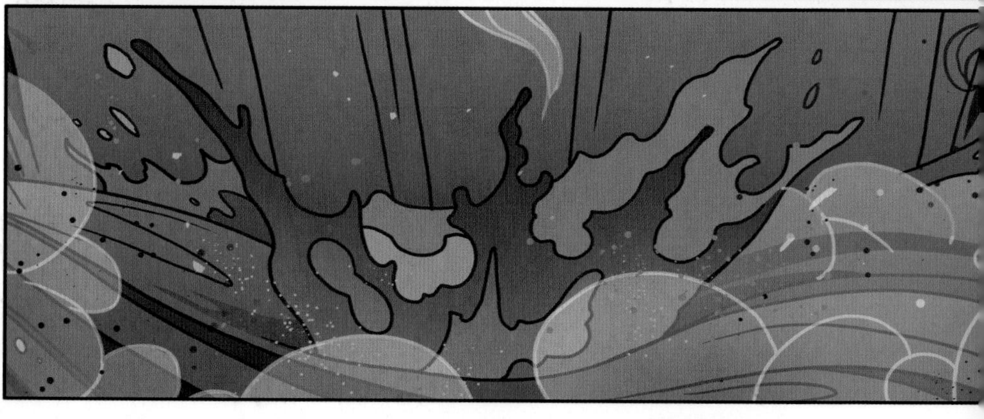

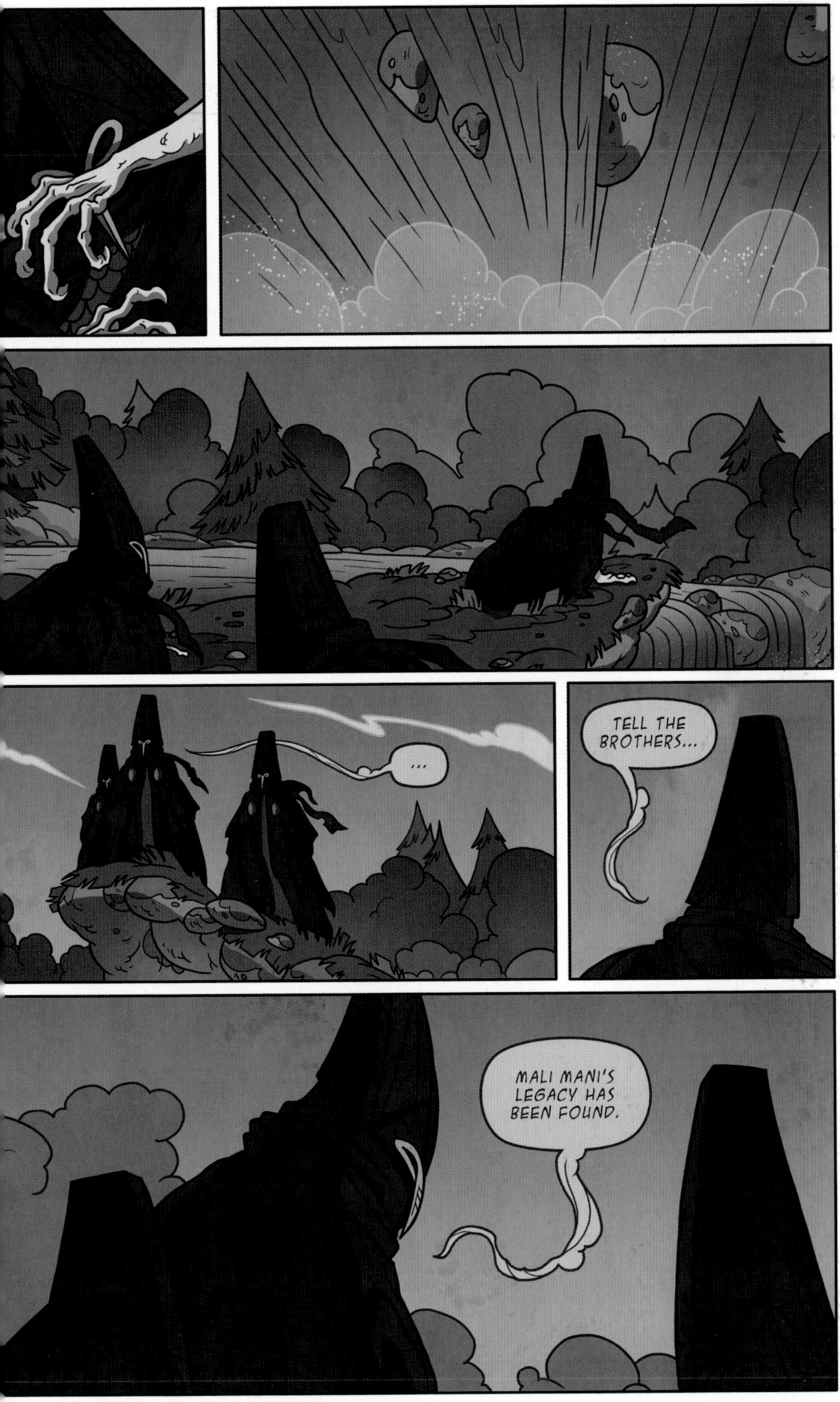
...
TELL THE BROTHERS...
MALI MANI'S LEGACY HAS BEEN FOUND.

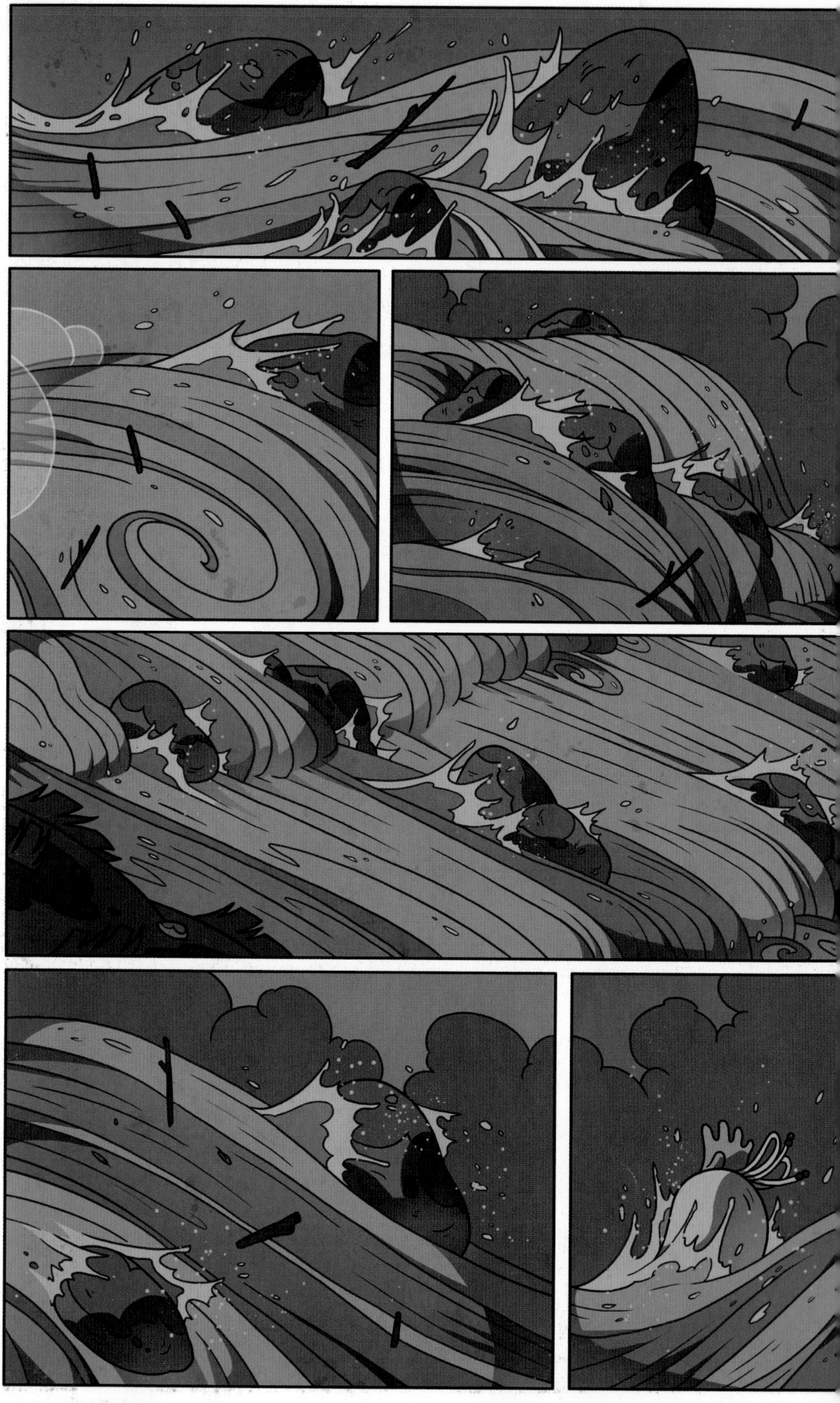

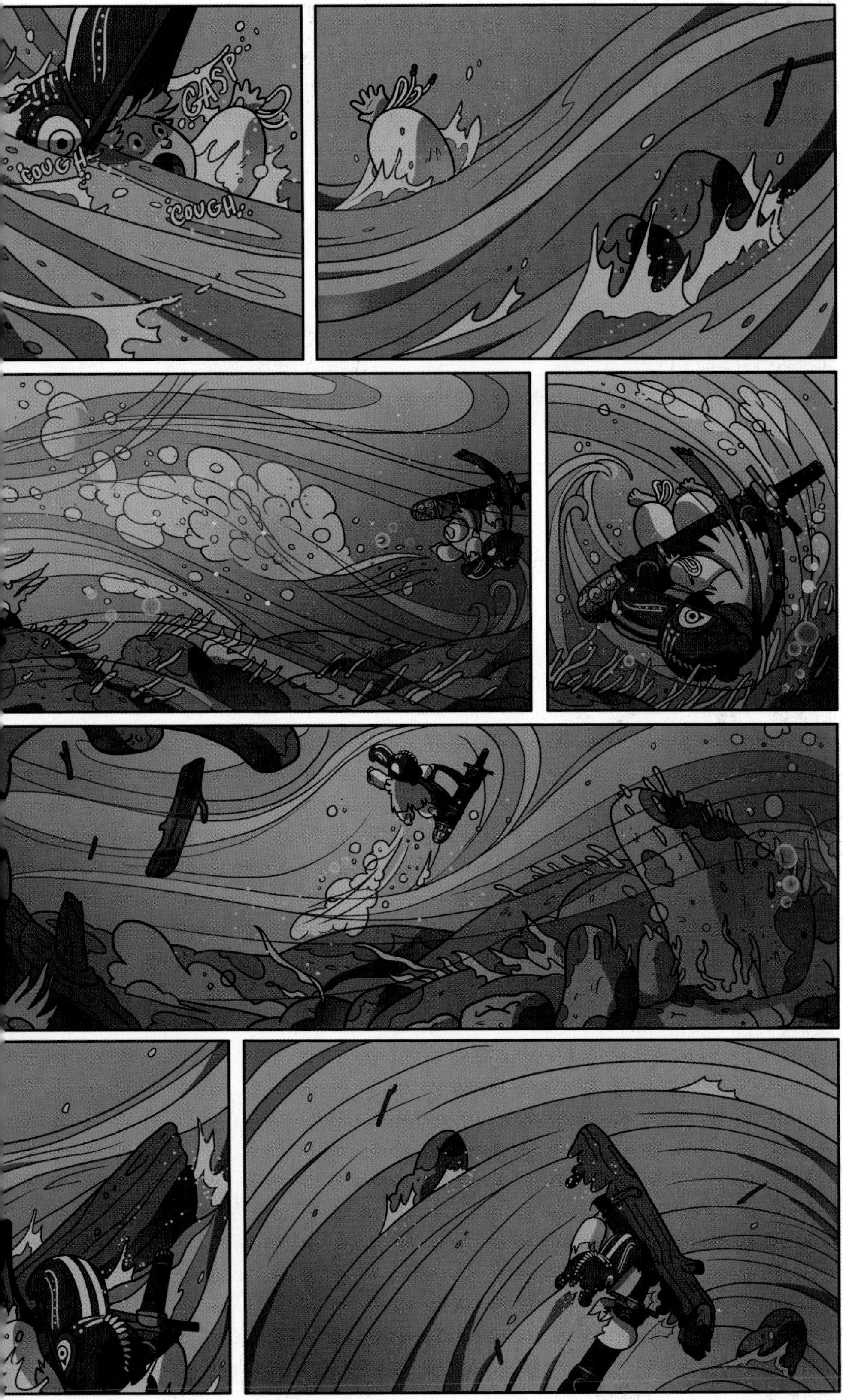
!!!
GASP
COUGH
COUGH

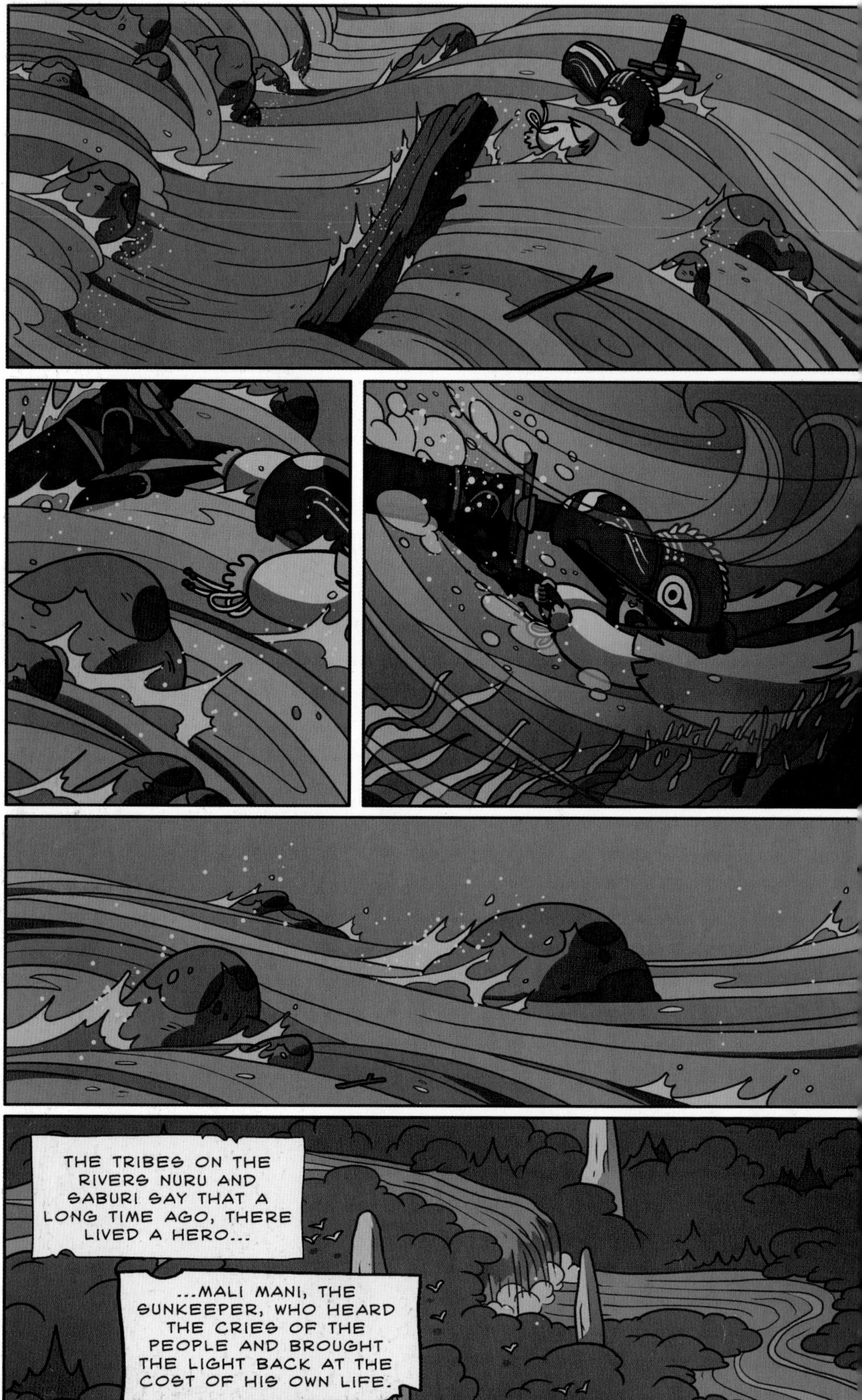
THE TRIBES ON THE RIVERS NURU AND SABURI SAY THAT A LONG TIME AGO, THERE LIVED A HERO...
...MALI MANI, THE SUNKEEPER, WHO HEARD THE CRIES OF THE PEOPLE AND BROUGHT THE LIGHT BACK AT THE COST OF HIS OWN LIFE.

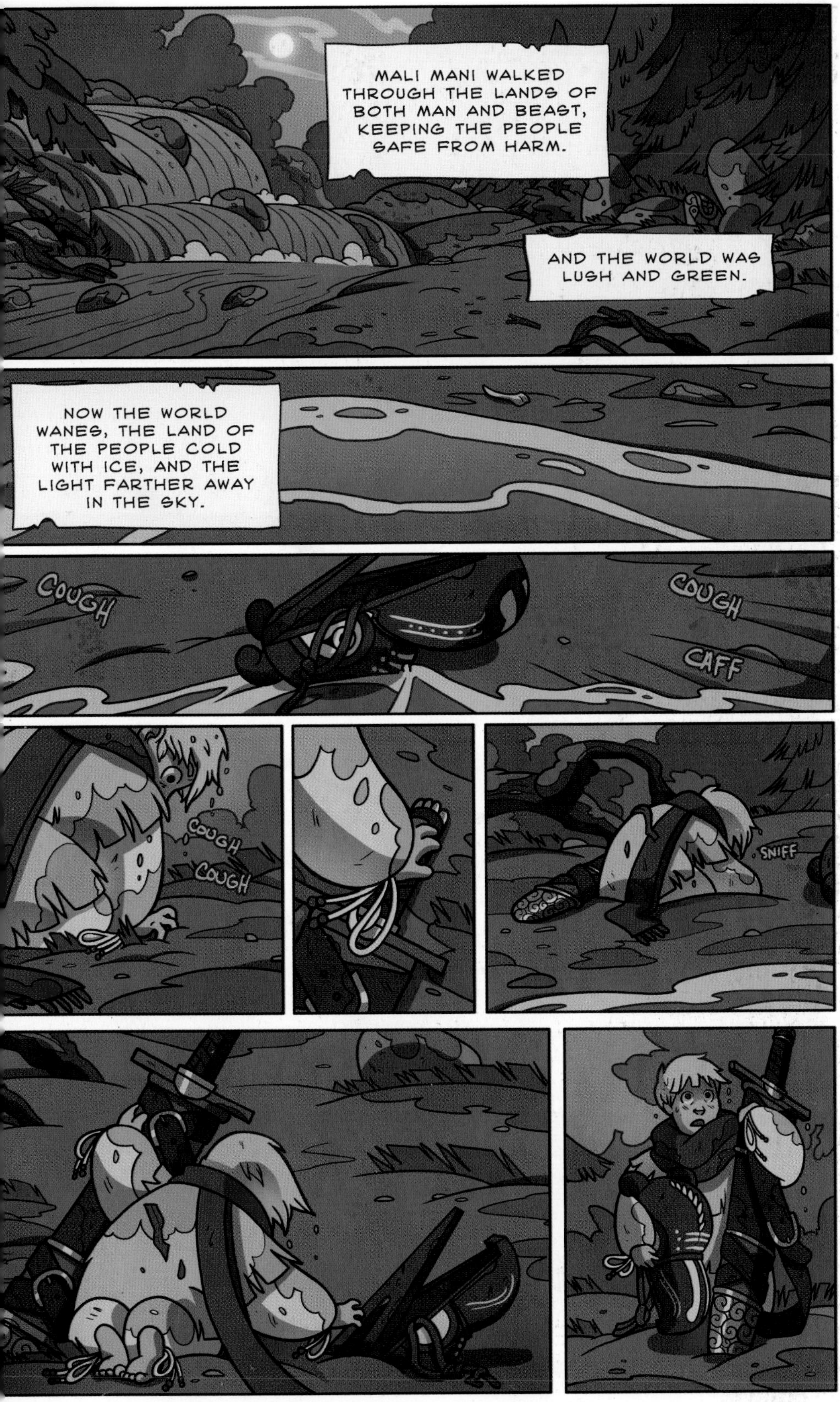
MALI MANI WALKED THROUGH THE LANDS OF BOTH MAN AND BEAST, KEEPING THE PEOPLE SAFE FROM HARM.
AND THE WORLD WAS LUSH AND GREEN.
NOW THE WORLD WANES, THE LAND OF THE PEOPLE COLD WITH ICE, AND THE LIGHT FARTHER AWAY IN THE SKY.
COUGH
COUGH
CAFF
COUGH
COUGH
SNIFF

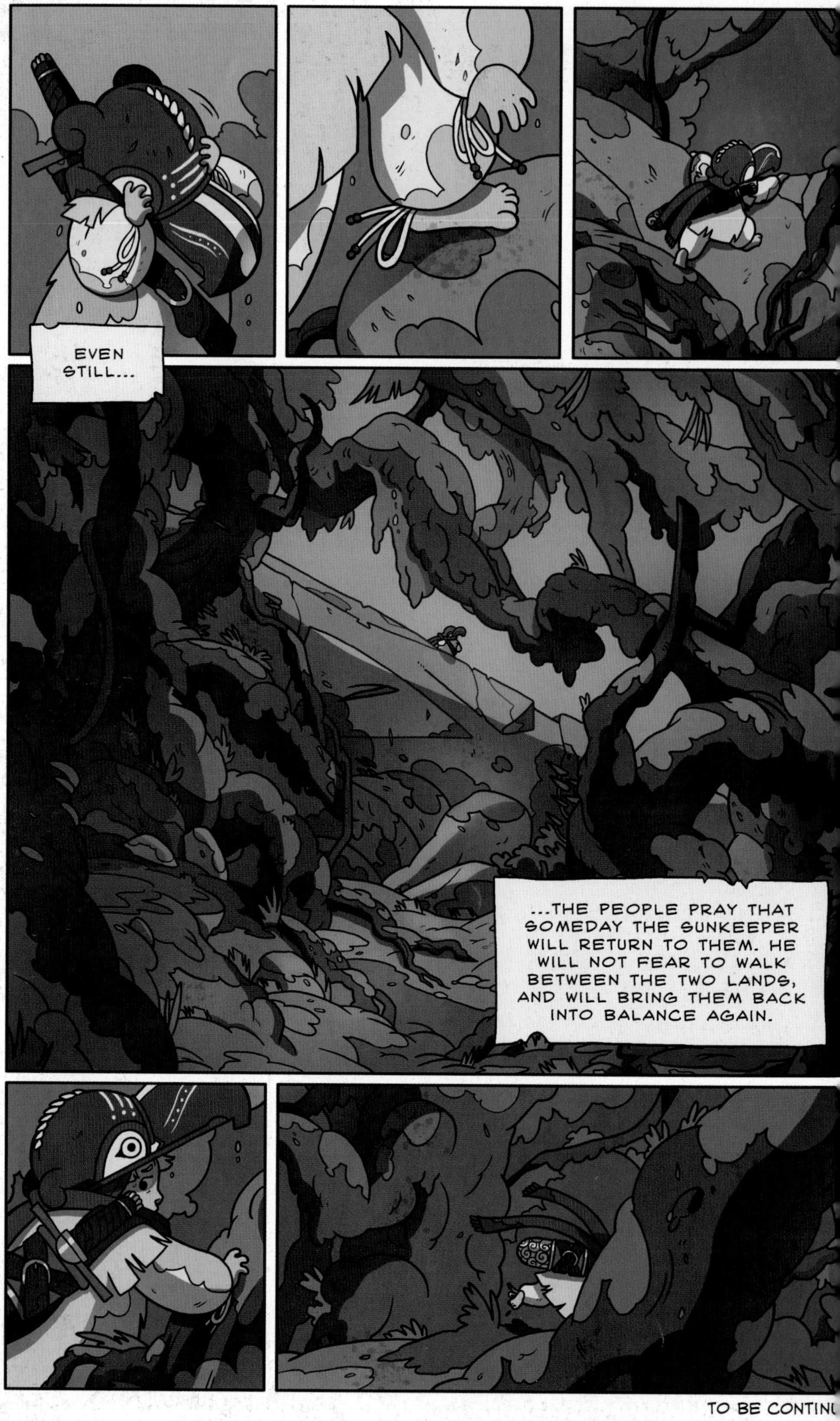
EVEN STILL...
...THE PEOPLE PRAY THAT SOMEDAY THE SUNKEEPER WILL RETURN TO THEM. HE WILL NOT FEAR TO WALK BETWEEN THE TWO LANDS, AND WILL BRING THEM BACK INTO BALANCE AGAIN.

TO BE CONTINU

BIRD·BOY

SKETCHBOOK

Notes by Anne Szabla

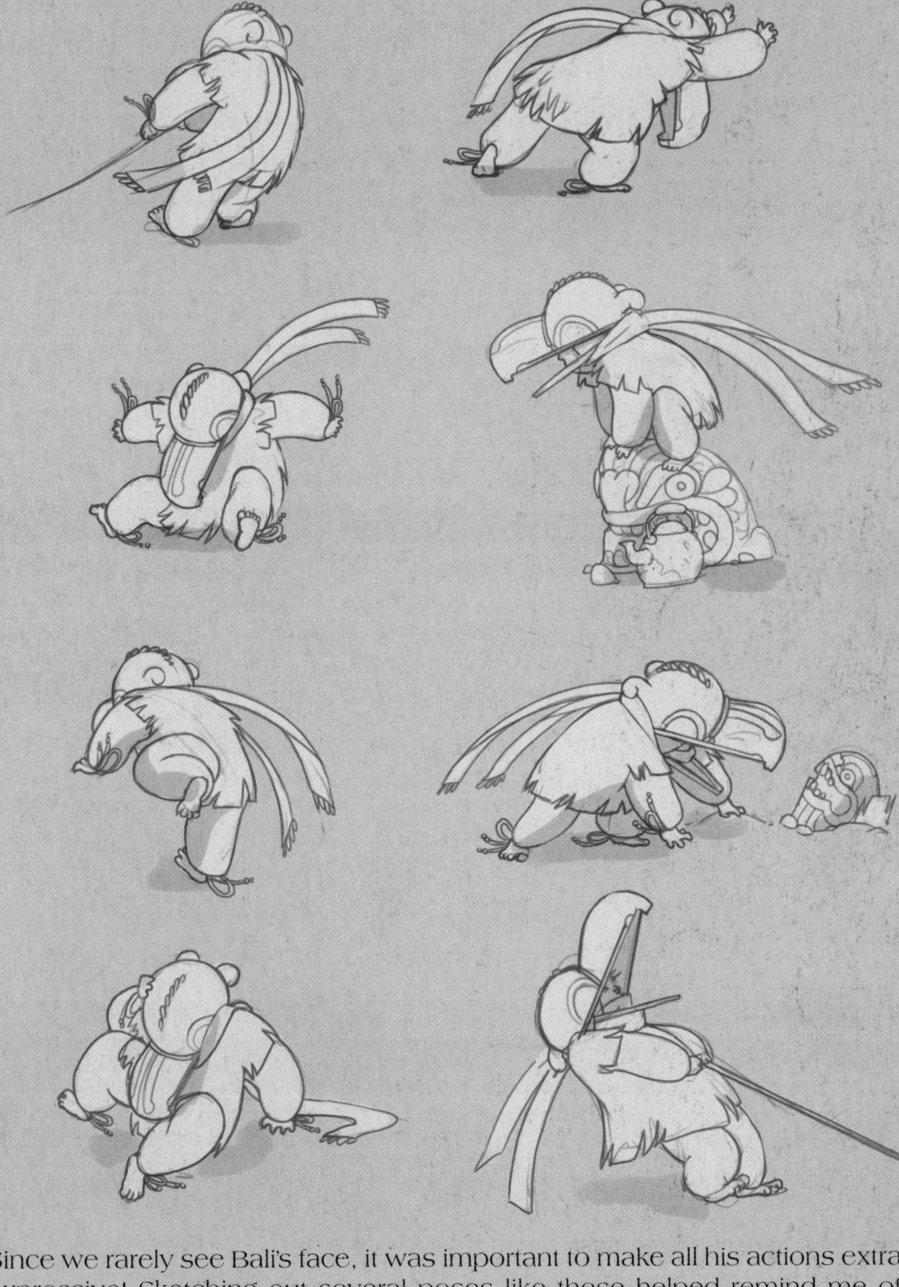

Since we rarely see Bali's face, it was important to make all his actions extra expressive! Sketching out several poses like these helped remind me of this when I went to draw the comic pages.

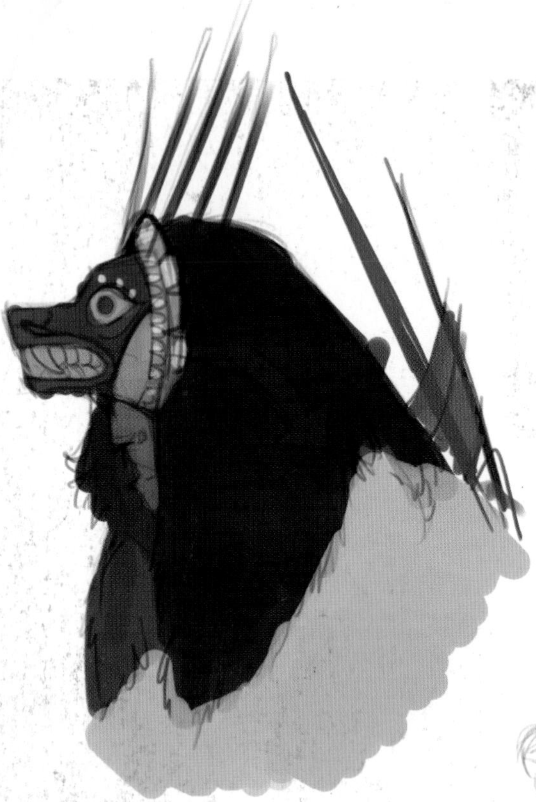

Some early ideas for the hunters.

Facing: A Rook!

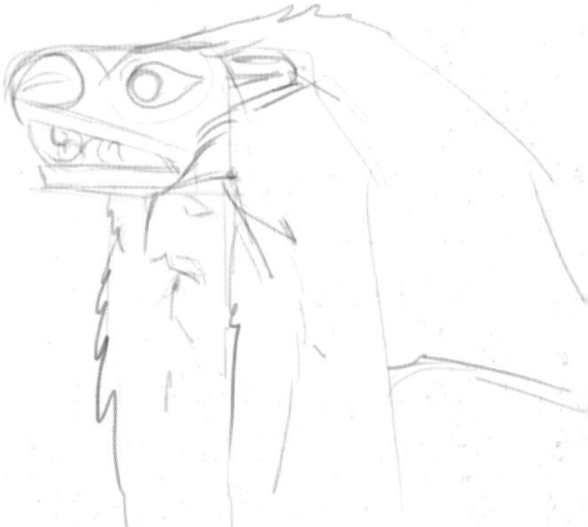

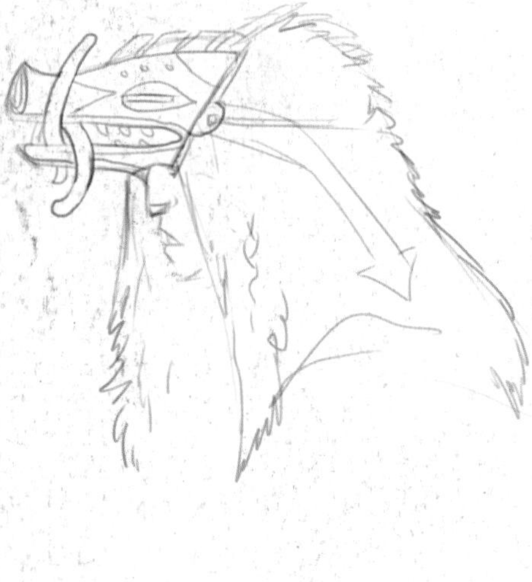

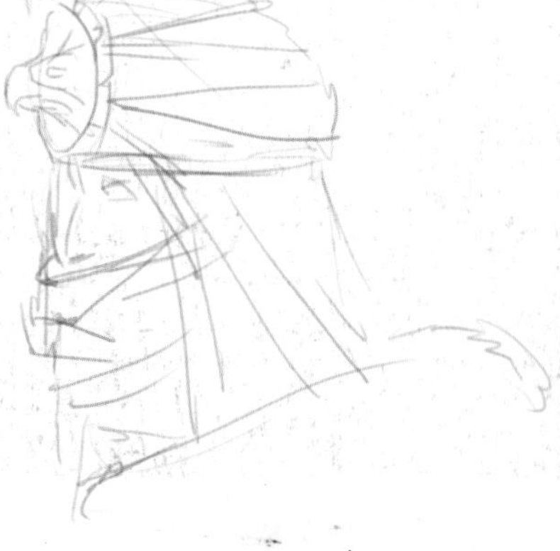

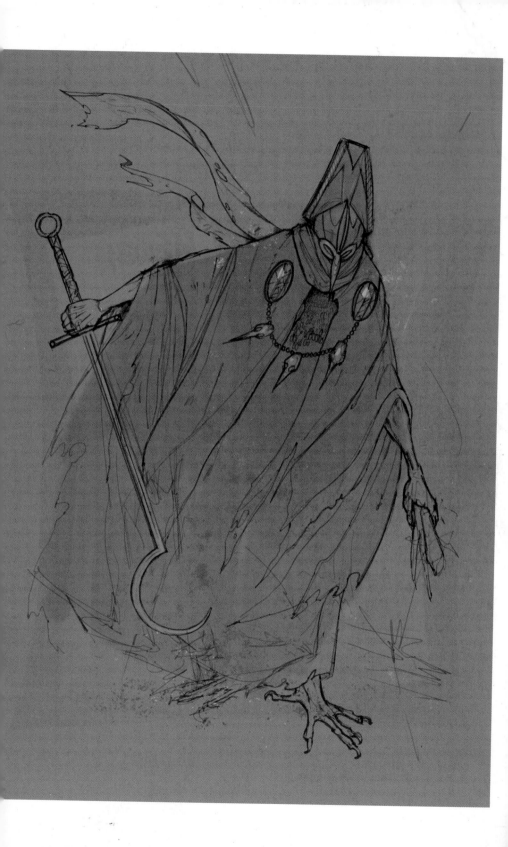

DISCOVER THE ADVENTURE!

Explore these beloved books for the entire family.

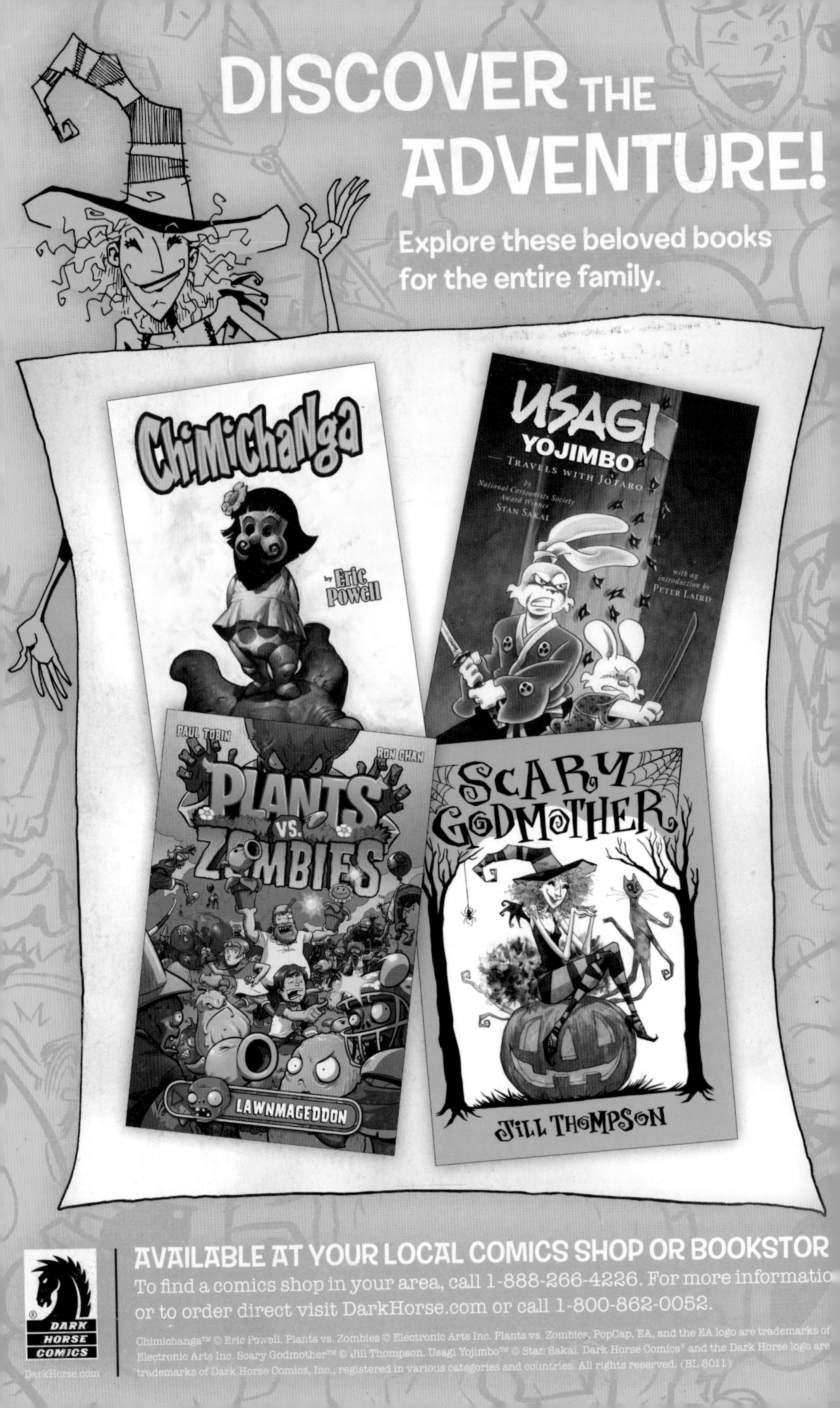

ChiMiChaNga
by Eric Powell
USAGI YOJIMBO
TRAVELS WITH JOTARO
by National Cartoonists Society Award Winner STAN SAKAI
with an introduction by PETER LAIRD
PAUL TOBIN
RON CHAN
PLANTS VS. ZOMBIES
LAWNMAGEDDON
SCARY GODMOTHER
JILL THOMPSON

AVAILABLE AT YOUR LOCAL COMICS SHOP OR BOOKSTOR

To find a comics shop in your area, call 1-888-266-4226. For more informatio or to order direct visit DarkHorse.com or call 1-800-862-0052.

DARK HORSE COMICS
DarkHorse.com